Daisy's Aunt

By

I0561787

E. F. BENSON

British Library Cataloguing-in-Publication Data
A catalogue record for this book is available from the
British Library

E.F. Benson

Edward Frederic Benson was born at Wellington College (where his father was headmaster) in Berkshire, England in 1867.He was educated at Marlborough College, where he proved himself as an excellent athlete, representing England at figure skating, and published his first novel, *Dodo* (1893), when he was 26.The novel was quite popular, and Benson eventually expanded it into a trilogy (*Dodo the Second*, in 1914, and *Dodo Wonders*, in 1921).Nowadays, Benson is principally known for his 'Mapp and Lucia' series about Emmeline "Lucia" Lucas and Elizabeth Mapp.The series consists of six novels and two short stories, and remains popular to this day, being serialized for Radio 4 as recently as 2008.Benson was also a respected writer of ghost stories – indeed, H. P. Lovecraft spoke very highly of him, especially his story 'The Man Who Went Too Far'.Benson died of throat cancer in 1940, aged 72.

CONTENTS

DAISY'S AUNT.

CHAPTER I.

Daisy Hanbury poked her parasol between the bars of the cage, with the amiable intention of scratching the tiger's back. The tiger could not be expected to know this all by himself, and so he savagely bit the end of it off, with diabolical snarlings. Daisy turned to her cousin with a glow of sympathetic pleasure.

"What a darling!" she said. "He didn't understand, you see, and was perfectly furious. And it cost pounds and pounds, and I've spent all my allowance, and so I can't buy another, and my complexion will go to the dogs. Let's go there, too; the dingoes are absolutely fascinating. We'll come back to see these angels fed."

Gladys laughed.

"Daisy, you have got the most admirable temper," she said. "I should have called that brute any names except 'darling' and 'angel.'"

"I know you would, because you don't understand either it or me. I understand both perfectly. You see, you don't love fierce wild things—things that are wicked and angry, and, above all, natural. I don't mind good, sweet, gentle things, like—oh, like almost everybody, if only they are sweet and good naturally. But generally they are not. Their sweetness is the result of education or morality, or something tedious, not the result of their natures, of themselves. Oh, I know all about it! Gladys, this parasol is beyond hope. Let's conceal it in the bushes like a corpse."

Daisy looked round with a wild and suspicious eye.

"There's a policeman," she said. "I'm sure he'll think that I have murdered my own parasol. Oh, kind Mr. Policeman—there, that softened him, and he's looking the other way."

Gladys gave a little shriek of dismay as Daisy thrust her parasol into a laurustinus.

"Oh! but the handle, and the ribs!" she cried. "It only wanted a new point, and—and to be recovered. Daisy, I never saw such extravagance. You mustn't leave it. I'll have it done up for you."

"That's angelic of you," said Daisy; "but will you carry it for me in the meantime? It's that that matters. I couldn't be seen going about even at the Zoo with a parasol in that condition. I should have to explain to everybody exactly how it happened, which would take time."

"But of course I'll carry it for you," said Gladys.

Daisy considered this noble offer.

"It's quite too wonderful of you," she said, "but I don't think I could be seen with you if you were carrying it. No; come to the dogs. Oh, Gladys, you are sweet and good and gentle quite, quite naturally, and I adore you."

The dingoes were rewarding, and Daisy instantly curried favour with their keeper, and learnt about their entrancing habits; afterwards the two went back to see the lions fed before leaving. The tiger which had ruined her parasol proved to have the most excellent appetite, which much relieved Daisy's mind, as she feared that the point, which he seemed to have completely eaten, might have spoilt his dinner. She hurried breathlessly down the line as the huge chops of raw meat were passed in and snatched up by the animals, absorbed and radiant. Gladys, as always, followed where the other led, but was conscious of qualms. These she concealed as best she could.

"Oh, I want to say grace for them all," said Daisy at the end. "I *do* hope they are pleased with their dinners.

Are the keepers fair, do you think? There was a dreadful amount of bone in my parasol-tiger's dinner, if you understand. Gladys, I don't believe you loved it. How stupid of you! You don't quite understand; you don't know how nice it is to be greedy instead of gentle. Do try. Oh, no, let's go out by this gate."

"But we shall have to walk miles before we get a cab," said Gladys.

"I know; that's why. It will make us late for Aunt Alice's tea-party. I hate tea-parties."

"But mother asked me to be back by five," said Gladys.

"Did she? Did she really?" asked Daisy.

"Indeed she did."

"Oh, well, then of course we'll drive back, though I did want to walk. But it can't possibly be helped. We must drive. It is such a pity not to do as you are asked. I always do, except when Willie asks me to marry him."

They got into their hansom and bowled silently down the dry grey road. All June was in flower in the pink pyramids of the chestnut-trees, and was already beginning to bleach the colour out of the long coarse grass in the open spaces of the Park. There swarms of girls and boys rioted ecstatically; here the more lucky, in possession of a battered bat and a ball begrimed with much honourable usage, had set up three crooked sticks to serve as wickets, and played with an enthusiasm that the conditions of the game might justly have rendered difficult of achievement. The one thing certain about the ball was that it would not come off the baked, uneven ground at the angle at which it might be expected. It might shoot, or on pitching might tower like a partridge, and any ball pitched off the wicket might easily take it; the only thing quite certain was that a straight ball (unless a full pitch) would not. Above, the thick dusky blue of a fine summer day in London formed a cloudless dome, where the sun still swung high on its westering course. In front of the distances that dusky pall was visible, and the houses at the edge of the Park were blurred in outline and made beautiful by the inimitable dinginess of the city.

But Gladys had no eye for all this; she was burning to know what was the latest development in the Willie affair, but her whole-hearted affection for her cousin was a little touched by timidity, and she did not quite like to question her. For Daisy, in spite of her charm, was a little formidable at times; at times she would have moods of entrancing tenderness; she could comfort or appeal, just as she could take the most sympathetic pleasure in the fact that a fierce tiger was annoyed at her amiable intentions, and had spoilt her best parasol. But at other times there was something of the tiger in her—that, no doubt, was why she understood this one so well—which made Gladys a little shy of her. She had often, so to speak, bitten off the end of her cousin's parasol before now, and Gladys did not appreciate that as much as Daisy had just done. So in silence she looked a little sideways at that brilliant, vivid face, flushed with the swift blood of its twenty-two years, that looked so eagerly from its dark grey eyes on to the activity of the playing children. But silences were generally short when Daisy was present, and she proceeded to unfold herself with rapidity and all the naturalness of which she deplored the lack in the gentle, good people.

"Oh! how they are enjoying themselves," she said, "with really no material at all. Gladys, think what a lot of material a person like me wants to make her enjoy herself! It really is shocking. My gracious, what an ugly child that is! Don't look at it; you never should look at ugly things—it's bad for the soul. Yes, I want such a lot to make me happy—all there is, in fact—and poor darling Willie hasn't got all there is. He's the sort of man I should like to marry when I am forty-three. Do you know what I mean? He would be quite charming if one were forty-three. He's quite charming now, if it comes to that, and I'm dreadfully fond of him, but he thinks about me too much; he's too devoted. I hear his devotion going on tick, tick, all the time, like the best clocks. That's one reason for not marrying him."

"I don't think it's a good one, though," remarked Gladys.

"Yes, it is. Because a man always expects from his wife what he gives her. He would be absolutely happy living with me on a desert island; but—I know it's true—he would tacitly require that I should be absolutely happy living with him on a desert island. Well, I shouldn't—I shouldn't—I shouldn't. I should not! Is that clear?"

"Quite."

"Very well, then, why did you say it wasn't? Oh, yes, I know I am right. And he would always see that I was well wrapped up, and wonder whether I wasn't a little pale. I can't bear that sort of thing. No doubt it's one way of love; but I must say I prefer another. I daresay the love that is founded on esteem and respect and affection is a very excellent thing, but it's one of those excellent things which I am quite willing to let other people have and enjoy. It's like—like Dresden china; I am sure it is quite beautiful, but I don't want any myself. I wish you would marry Willie yourself, darling. Don't mind me."

They rattled out over the cobblestones of the gate into Baker Street, and plunged into the roaring traffic. Daisy had still a great deal to say, and she raised her voice to make it heard above the intolerable clatter of motor 'buses and the clip-clop of horses' hoofs.

"Besides, as I said, I want such a lot of things. I'm hard and worldly and disgusting; but so it is. I want to be right at the top of the tree, and if I married Willie I should just be Mrs. Carton, with that decaying old place in Somerset; very nice and intensely respectable, but that's all. It's quite a good thing to be nice and respectable, but it's rather a vegetable thing to be, if you are nothing else. I must be an animal at least, and that's why I'm playing 'Animal Grab.'"

Gladys looked—as was indeed the case—as if she did not quite understand this surprising statement.

"I'm very slow, I know," she said, "but——"

"Yes, darling, you are, but you do know what I mean, though you don't know you know it. I've often seen you wondering about it. Oh, that motor 'bus is going to run into us! It isn't; how can you be so nervous? It cleared us by at least a quarter of an inch. Yes, 'Animal Grab.' Now 'yes' or 'no,' do you know what I mean, or don't you?"

Gladys trembled under these direct assaults. But she thought "yes" was more likely to be favourably received than "no," and so allowed herself to say "yes."

But it proved to be a vain hope that Daisy would thereupon go on and explain. That was so like Daisy; she never did what you hoped or expected she might. Gladys on this occasion, with her pink, timorous face and general air of discouragement, prayed that Daisy might not trouble about her, but just go on talking. It is true that Daisy did talk next, but, instead of expounding, she rapped out a question.

"So you do know," she said. "Then what is it?"

Gladys shut her eyes for a moment to encourage bravery.

"I suppose it means that you are thinking whether you will marry Lord Lindfield or not," she said.

Daisy, however peremptory, was not a bully.

"How did you guess that, dear?" she asked.

"It wasn't very difficult. It couldn't have been, you see, or I shouldn't have guessed it. But he has been— well, a good deal interested in you, hasn't he, and you— —"

"Do you mean I've encouraged him?" asked Daisy, with an inquisitorial air.

"No, I mean just the opposite. You've rather snubbed him." Gladys made a huge demand on her courage. "But you've snubbed him in such a way that it comes to the same thing as if you had encouraged him," she said.

Daisy considered this.

"I think you've got a horrid mind, Gladys," she said at length. "If I encourage somebody you tell me I am flirting, and if I discourage him you tell me it comes to the same thing. And you do me an injustice. I haven't snubbed or discouraged him. I've—I've remained neutral, until I could make up my mind. Do you think he cares for me? I really don't know whether he does or not. I can always tell with the gentle, good people like Willie, and it is gentle, good people whom I see most. Oh!"

Daisy gave a great sigh, and leant out over the folded door of the hansom.

"I'm not sure if I want to marry Lord Lindfield or not," she said, "but I'm perfectly certain that I don't want him to marry anybody else. I think I should like him always to remain wanting to marry me, while I didn't want to marry him. I'm dreadfully glad you think that I can snub or encourage him, because that means that you think he cares. I should be perfectly miserable if I thought he didn't."

"I don't think you need be miserable," said Gladys.

"I'm not. Oh, there's the Prime Minister; I shall bow. That was a failure. He looked at me like a fish. How rude the Cabinet makes people! The Cabinet always goes about with the British Empire pick-a-back. At least, it thinks the British Empire is pick-a-back. The Empire doesn't. About Lord Lindfield. He's turning grey over the temples, and I think that is so frightfully attractive. Of course, he's awfully old; he must be nearly forty. He's dining to-night, isn't he? Then I shall arrange the table. Yes, you needn't look like that. I shan't make him take me in. He's supposed to be wicked, too. Oh, Gladys, it is so nice if men go playing about, and then fall in love with me. It's worth heaps of the other kind.

Oh, don't look shocked; it is silly to look shocked, and so easy."

The hansom waited for a moment at the junction of Orchard Street and Oxford Street, and the innumerable company of locomotives sped by it. Motors shot by with a whirr and a bubbling, hansoms jingled westwards, large slow vans made deliberate progress, delaying the traffic as some half-built dam impedes the course of flowing water till it finds a way round it, and through the streams of wheels and horses pedestrians scuttled in and out like bolted rabbits. The whole tide of movement was at its height, and the little islands in mid-street were crowded with folk who were cut off, it would seem, by the rising flood-water from all communication with the shore, with but remote chance of escape. Then an omnipotent policeman stepped out into the surging traffic, held up a compelling and resistless hand, and at his gesture the tides, more obedient to him than to Canute, ceased to flow, and the cross-movement began, which permitted Daisy and her cousin to cross the stream. But whether it was that the stoppage in their passage made a corresponding halt in her thoughts, or whether, as was more likely, she had said all that she meant to say on the subject of Lord Lindfield, she began, just as they started to move again, on something widely different.

"And Aunt Jeannie comes to-morrow," she said, "which is quite delightful. For I do believe I've missed her every single day since she went away a year ago. And if I do that, you may depend upon it that she is very nice indeed. As a rule, I like people very much when they are there, and I get along excellently without them when they are not."

"Quite—quite true," said Gladys, with a touch of acidity.

"It's much the most sensible plan," continued Daisy, perceiving, but completely ignoring, the tone. "It does no good to miss people, and, as I say, I seldom do it. But I always miss Aunt Jeannie. I should like to see her every day of my life. It would be dreadful to see most people every day, though I like them so much when I do see them. Oh, Gladys darling, don't look as if you were in church! You can't take things lightly, you know."

"And you can't take them in any other way," remarked Gladys.

"Oh, but I can; it is only that I don't usually choose to. It is a great blessing I don't take every one seriously. If I took Willie seriously, I should find him a great bore; as it is, I think he is quite charming, and I should certainly marry him if I were fifty."

"It was forty-three just now," said Gladys.

"Yes; but being with you has made me grow older very quickly," said Daisy.

Gladys laughed; with Daisy it was very true that "c'est le ton qui fait la musique," and the same words which in another tone could have wounded her, now merely amused. It had taken her a long time to get used, so to speak, to this brilliant, vivid friend, who turned such an engaging smile on the world in general, and shone with supreme impartiality on the wicked and the good, and to know her, as she knew her now, with greater thoroughness than she knew herself. Ethically, if Gladys had been put to the question on her oath, she would have had to give the most unsatisfactory account of her friend, and, to sum up all questions in one, it would have come to this—that she believed Daisy to be quite heartless. But, humanly, there was in Daisy much to take the place of that profound organ. She had the joy of life and the interest in life to a supreme degree, and though she resolutely turned her back on anything disagreeable or ugly, her peremptory dismissal of such things was more than made up for by her unbounded welcome of all that pleased her. You had only to please her (and she was very ready to be pleased), and she poured sunlight on you. And Gladys, who was naturally rather shy, rather slow to make friends, rather reticent, soon grasped this essential fact about Daisy, and having grasped it, held tightly to it. She felt she would not readily go to Daisy if she was in trouble, but there was no one to whom she would hurry with such certainty of welcome if she was happy. And though, no doubt, sympathy, to be complete, must feel for sorrow as keenly as it feels for joy, yet a nature that feels keenly for joy and turns its back on sorrow is perhaps quite as fine a one as that which, though it may be an excellent comforter, is rather of the nature of a wet blanket when a happy soul appeals to it for sympathy. And on joy, whether her own or that of another, Daisy never turned her back. She delighted in the happiness of others.

CHAPTER II.

Daisy's father and mother had both died when she was quite young, and not yet half-way through the momentous teens. For seven years after that she had lived with her mother's sister, the inimitable Aunt Jeannie, whom she wished to see every day. But though she had passed seven years with her, she had barely seen her aunt's husband. It was his death, a year ago, that had sent her to the Nottinghams, for Aunt Jeannie in a crisis of nerves had been ordered abroad for a year, and was now on the point of return, and, having returned, was to stay with Lady Nottingham for the indefinite period which may be taken up by the finding of a suitable house.

Daisy knew there had been trouble at the back of all this. Uncle Francis, Aunt Jeannie's husband, had been called an invalid, and she gathered that his ill-health was something not to be openly alluded to. Morphia was connected with it, a "habit" was connected with it, and since this was somehow disagreeable, she had long ago so successfully banished it from her thoughts that her curiosity about it was a thing without existence. Certainly he made Aunt Jeannie very unhappy, but Aunt Jeannie, who was such a dear, and so young still—not more than thirty, for she was the youngest of a family of whom Daisy's mother was the eldest—had been always sedulous to hide disquietude from her niece. And it was entirely characteristic of Daisy to be grateful for having it all hid from her, and not even in thought to conjecture what it was all about. During this year of separation from Aunt Jeannie, in which, as she had said (and Daisy, with all her faults and limitations, was a George Washington for truth), she had missed her every day, she had always looked forward to her return, and, though she liked being with Lady Nottingham very much, knew that she would ultimately go back to the unrivalled other aunt again with the intensest satisfaction.

But of late the prospect of going back, or living with any aunt at all, had receded into at least a middle distance. There was no doubt in her own mind (though she liked the absence of doubt to be endorsed by her cousin) that Lord Lindfield had been extremely attentive to her for the last month or so. He had committed dreadful social crimes, such as throwing over an engagement already made and nearly due, when he found that she would be at some house to which he was subsequently invited. And somehow (that was the charm of him, or part or it), though he upset dinner-tables right and left, nobody really minded. Match-making London, which includes the larger part of that marriageable city, even when they were personally affronted and inconvenienced, smiled sympathetically when they heard what his movements on the night he ought to have dined with them had been. He did even worse than that; he had once, indeed, omitted to send the excuse of a subsequent engagement, and everybody had waited a quarter of an hour for him to put in a belated appearance. And when he did not his hostess had remarked that he must be "picking daisies," and the procession had gone dinner-wards with a widowed girl.

It turned out to be true, did this conjecture of the hostess. He had dined "quietly" that night at Lady Nottingham's, and had played "old maid" afterwards, as bridge was universally voted to be far too intellectual. And Daisy took huge pleasure in such facts as these, stealthily conveyed to her by one if not more of her innumerable girl friends. For though there was no doubt that many dutiful mothers would have liked their daughters to marry Lord Lindfield, yet when he declared himself by signs as unmistakable as this, they neither felt nor communicated any ill-humour.

He was picking daisies; very well, the sooner he plucked the particular one the better. Daisy was so pleasant; no wonder, after all, that he wished for her. And she too, quite soon, would join the ranks of the match-makers, and be immensely kind to everybody else.

Yet if only Katie or Elsie or Nellie——— But it was no use thinking about that. Daisy, once settled, would certainly do her best for those to whom fortune must pay a "subsequent" visit.

Lady Nottingham purred approval over the girls on their punctual return, before any of her guests had arrived. She was rather stout and very comfortable. Behind her stoutness and her comfort there beat a heart of gold, and an extremely acute brain, which was not always allowed for, was alert and watchful. A heart of gold is considered as not incompatible with comfort and stoutness, but nobody who had not come to grips with her, or been her ally in some affair that called for diplomacy or tact, knew how excessively efficient her brain was. She had, too, the supreme gift of only sending into action as much of it as was required to do the work, and never made elaborate plans when something simple would do as well.

All this combined to make not only a character that was lovable, but a friend whose wisdom might be depended on, and Daisy was eminently right in valuing her aunt's counsel and advice. She sought it, indeed, this evening, in the quiet half-hour that intervened between the departure of the tea-party guests and the time when it was necessary to dress for dinner.

Lady Nottingham was resting in her room when Daisy went to her, ostensibly (and quite truly) to get the list of those who were coming to dinner that night in order to arrange the table. But though she would have gone there in any case for that reason, another and far more essential one lay behind it. She wanted, indeed, to get her aunt's opinion on the point she had herself talked to Gladys about that afternoon, and sound her as to her opinion about Lord Lindfield.

The sorting of people to see who would take whom in to dinner, with abstracted frownings over the map of the table, seemed to Daisy an admirable accompaniment for disjointed questions, and one which would give her an adventitious advantage, since at any moment she could be absorbed in the task she was so kindly occupying herself with, and be silent over it, if a reply was in any way inconvenient.

This sort of diplomacy, though not exactly habitual with Daisy, seemed to her sufficiently acute and blinding, and she sat on the floor with a peerage, the list of the guests, a sheet of paper and a pencil, and began at once, while Lady Nottingham "rested" on the sofa against which Daisy leant her back.

"Oh, what nice people!" said Daisy. "Can't they all take me in? Willie Carton, Jimmie, Lord Lindfield, Mr. Braithwaite, and Lord Pately. Dear Willie! I suppose he ought to take me in. Do you mind whether you sit at the end of the table or in the middle of the middle, Aunt Alice? Middle of the middle always works out more easily. All right. Dear Willie!"

The diplomat, who is known to be a diplomat, is at once under a heavy handicap. Daisy was instantly detected, and Lady Nottingham, since there was no direct question to reply to, preserved silence. Then, after a sufficient pause, she asked,—

"Have you settled about Willie, dear?"

"Ye-es. It will be better if he takes Gladys in."

"Then he's settled for," said Lady Nottingham, turning over a page in her book.

This did not suit Daisy; she had meant to make Aunt Alice ask leading questions, instead of which she only gave the most prosaic answers. She sighed.

"Poor Willie!" she said.

Aunt Alice laughed quietly and comfortably.

"Dearest Daisy," she said, "as you want to tell me about Willie, why don't you do so? I suppose you want me to ask instead. Very well, it makes no difference. I imagine he has proposed again to you, and that you have refused him, and want to be quite sure I think you are wise about it. You see, you said, 'Dear Willie' first, and 'Poor Willie' afterwards. What other inference could a reasonable woman like me draw? If you hadn't wanted to talk about it, you would have said neither the one nor the other. Hadn't you better begin?"

Daisy laughed.

"I think you are a witch," she said. "Oh, one moment; the table is coming right. Yes, and me at the end."

"And Lord Lindfield on your left," said Lady Nottingham, without looking up.

That was the end of Daisy's diplomacy.

"You would have been burnt at the stake two hundred years ago, darling Aunt Alice," she said. "I should have helped to pile the faggots."

"What a good thing I wasn't born earlier," said she. Then for a moment she thought intently; what she wanted to say next required consideration. "Daisy dear," she said, "I wanted to talk to you also, and if you had not been so very diplomatic I should have begun."

"Oh, I wish I had waited," said Daisy.

"Yes. But it makes no difference. What you want is my advice to you as to whether you should accept Lord Lindfield. I quite agree with you that he is going to propose to you. Otherwise he has been flirting with you disgracefully, and I have never known him flirt with a girl before."

Lady Nottingham put her book quite completely down. She wanted to convey certain things quite clearly but without grossness.

"Now, Daisy, you are very young," she said, "but in some ways you are extremely grown-up. I mean, I think you know your own mind very well. I wish very much that your Aunt Jeannie had come back sooner, because she is about nine times as wise as I, and could have advised you instead of me. As it is, since I think you may have to settle a very important question any day, I have got to give you the best advice I can. I think he will propose to you, as I said, any day; indeed, I feel quite certain of it, else it would be abominable in me to talk to you about it at all. Therefore, do make up your mind before he does. Don't say, when he does, that you are not sure, that you must take time to consider it. There is no reason why a girl should not say 'yes' or 'no' at once, unless the question comes as an entire surprise, which it does not do except in second-rate novels like this one."

Lady Nottingham dropped the condemned volume on the floor.

"In real life," she said, "every girl sees long before a man proposes whether he is likely to do so, and should know quite well what she is going to say. And I think you intend to say 'yes.' You must, however, be quite sure that, as far as you can tell, you are making a wise choice.

"Now, I am not going to shock you, but very likely I am going to make you think you are shocked. You are not really. The fact is, you are not in love with him, but he attracts you with an attraction that is very often in the same relation to love as the bud is to the flower. He has the sort of attraction for you that often contains the folded immature petals of the full flower. You wanted to ask me some series of questions which would lead up to that answer. And then you wanted to ask me one further question, which was whether that was enough to say 'yes' on. And my answer to that is 'yes.'"

The diplomacy in Daisy was quite completely dead. All this, so easy to the mature woman, seemed a sort of conjuring-trick to her. It was thought-reading of the most advanced kind, the reading of thoughts that she had not consciously formulated. And the soothsayer proceeded:—

"You have seen the advantages of such a marriage clearly enough. You are ambitious, my dear, you want to have a big position, to have big houses and plenty of money, and to take no thought of any material morrow. That is an advantage; it is only the stupid people, who call their stupidity unworldly, who think otherwise. But the great point is not to keep 'to-morrow' comfortable, but to keep an everlasting 'to-day.' You must be sure of that. Whatever the years bring—and Heaven knows what they will bring—you should feel now, when you consider whether you will accept him or not, that they can bring no difference to you. You must be unable to conceive of yourself at seventy as different from yourself now with regard to him. What is that music-hall song? 'We've been together now for forty years.' It expresses exactly what a girl should feel forty years before.

"And now for a thing more difficult to say. Lord Lindfield has—has knocked about a good deal. Sooner or later you will know that, and it is infinitely better that you should know it sooner, for it seems to me almost criminal that girls should be left to find that sort of thing out for themselves when it is too late. Mind, I do not say that he will knock about again. The fact that he is quite certainly intending to propose to you shows that he does not mean to. But he is not bringing a boy's first love to a girl."

Lady Nottingham leant forward and stroked Daisy's head.

"My dear, how brutal this must sound," she said. "But I am the least brutal of women. Assure yourself of that. And I have told you all there is to tell, as far as I know, but I should have blamed myself if I had told you less. And here is Hendon, and it is time for us to dress."

Daisy got up and kissed her aunt with a quick, trembling caress.

"I think you are a perfect darling," she said.

CHAPTER III.

The Dover boat, midday service, was on the point of starting from the quay at Calais, and luggage was being swung on to it in square trucks, the passengers having already embarked. The day before a midsummer storm had vexed the soul of the silver streak, which had turned to a grey pewter streak of a peculiarly streaky nature, with white tops to the waves that slung themselves over the head of the pier. Cabin-boys and stewards were making horrible dispositions of tinware, and the head steward was on the verge of distraction, since the whole world seemed to have chosen this particular day to return to England, and the whole world, with an eye on the Channel, desired private cabins, which were numerically less than the demand. At the moment he was trying to keep calm before the infuriated questions of a Frenchwoman who believed herself to be speaking English.

"Mais que faire?" she said. "I have ordered, and where is it? It is not, you tell me. I cannot be seeck with the canaille on the deck. I wish reservée. If not, I shall not go, and charge the company."

"Yes'm," said the steward. "Cabin-ticket, ma'am? Cabin No. 9. Show the lady to cabin No. 9."

Cabin No. 9 had heard these volubilities with sympathy, and a little secret amusement impossible to avoid if one were ever so little humorous, and lingered a moment while her maid went on to the cabin followed by a porter carrying small luggage.

"But I demand a cabin," continued this deeply-wronged lady. "C'est mon droit, si je la demande. Where is the capitan? Fetch him to me. Bring him. Oh, mon Dieu, the deck—to be seeck on the deck!"

Mrs. Halton, who was No. 9, called to her maid, and then spoke to the Frenchwoman.

"But I will gladly let you have my cabin," she said. "I do not mind the sea. I shall be quite happy on deck. Indeed it is no kindness. Very likely I should not have gone into my cabin at all."

The poor lady nearly wept with joy, and would willingly have paid Mrs. Halton ten times the amount the private cabin had cost; but that lady refused to make a start in trading at this time in her life, and having secured a sheltered corner watched for a little the inboarding of the passengers, but soon lost herself in her own reflections.

Ah, but how pleasant they were! She was coming home after a year abroad which had begun in widowhood and loneliness and misery and shattered health, and was now returning, restored and comforted, to her friends and all that made life so engrossingly pleasant a business. No one deserved friends more thoroughly than she, and she was rich in that priceless capital of human affection. Sorrows and trials she had had in plenty in her life, but these the sweetness of her nature had transformed, so that from being things difficult to bear, she had built up with them her own character. Sorrow had increased her own power of sympathy; out of trials she had learnt patience; and failure and the gradual sinking of one she had loved into the bottomless slough of evil habit had but left her with an added dower of pity and tolerance.

So the past had no sting left, and if iron had ever entered into her soul it now but served to make it strong. She was still young, too; it was not near sunset with her yet, nor even midday, and the future that, humanly speaking, she counted to be hers was almost dazzling in its brightness. For love had dawned for her again, and no uncertain love, wrapped in the mists of memory, but one that had ripened through liking and friendship and intimacy into the authentic glory. He was in England, too; she was going back to him. And before very long she would never go away from him again.

Her place on deck had been wisely chosen, and, defended by the row of cabins at her back, she could watch in a dry windlessness the jovial riot of the seas. Now the steamer would stagger to some cross-blow of the waves; now, making a friend of them, swerved into a trough of opalescent green, and emerged again to take, like some fine-spirited horse, the liquid fence, flecked with bubbles, that lay in its course. The wind that had raised this gale still blew from the westward, and on the undefended deck great parcels of water, cut off from their seas, fell in solid lumps that resolved themselves into hissing streams.

And Daisy—Daisy occupied no small portion of her thoughts. A year ago she was on the threshold of womanhood, and at such critical periods Aunt Jeannie knew well that a year may confirm existing tendencies or completely alter them, bringing to light strands of character that had been woven below the surface. For many reasons she had a peculiar tenderness towards this dear niece. For seven rather dreadful years Daisy had lived with her, and during these Jeannie had never remitted her efforts to conceal from her that which had darkened her own life.

She believed (quietly, under her breath) that those efforts had been successful; she hoped anyhow that Daisy did not know of, did not even guess at, the underlying tragedy. For Daisy, all these years, had been in the seedtime of her life, and Mrs. Halton, rightly or wrongly, quite firmly believed that the young years of those who are to become men and women are best spent if during them they can be brought to learn the joy of life, while its possible tragedies are kept as far from them as may be. For, in general, the habit of joy is the best weapon with which to fight sorrow when sorrow comes. To expect the best of everything and everybody, and to go on doing so, is the best antidote for disappointments. To expect the worst, to think that disappointment is the usual outcome, is to be already unnerved for it. Life is best encountered with a sanguine heart.

Such, at any rate, was the creed of her who sat now on the deck of this labouring steamer as it ploughed its passage home, where were her friends and her lover. The tarpaulin had proved unnecessary, for she was sheltered by the deck-buildings from spray. Her book was also unnecessary, for she was more congenially occupied in this pleasant web of thought, and she sat there in her big fur cloak—for the wind of their motion made the air feel cold—with eyes that looked outwards, yet brooded inwardly, April-eyes, that were turned towards the summer that was coming. And all the past was poured into that, even as the squalls and tempests of winter are transmuted into and feed the luxuriance of June-time. The sorrow and the pain that were past had become herself; they were over, but their passage had left her more patient, more tolerant, more loving.

The deck was nearly empty, and but few of the more valiant walked up and down the sheltered swaying boards; but these, as often as they passed, looked again at her. Her mouth and chin were half lost and buried in the furry collar of her cloak, but above them was that fine, straight nose, just a little tip-tilted, the great brown eyes, and black hair growing low on the brow. Had her mouth been visible, a man would have said, "This is a woman," but without that he would very likely have said, "This is a girl," so young and so full of expectancy was her face. Yet had he looked twice at eyes and smooth, flushed cheeks alone, he would have said, "This is a woman," for though the joy of life beamed so freshly in her eyes, behind that there lurked something of its transmuted sorrows. Her expectancy was not that of ignorance; she knew, and still looked forward.

Under the lee of the English shore the sea abated, and she came on to the top deck from which they would disembark, and looked eagerly along the pier, telling herself that her expectations that she would see a certain figure there were preposterous, and yet cherishing them with a secret conviction. And then she knew that they were not preposterous at all; that it could not have been otherwise. Of course he had come down to Dover to meet her, and as she left the boat she was taken into his charge at once.

"Oh, Victor, how nice of you," she said. "I didn't expect you would come all the way down here a bit."

He held her hand, "but as long as all may, or so very little longer." But there was much that passed between them in that "very little longer."

"Nor did I expect to come," he said. "I only came."

She smiled at him.

"Ah, that's so like you," she said.

They waited with talk of commonplaces as to her journey and the crossing till Jeannie's maid came off the boat with her attendant baggage-bearer, and then went towards the train. They were the sort of people to whom a railway guard always touches his cap, and this duly occurred. Victor Braithwaite, however, had on this occasion already been in consultation with him, and they were taken to a compartment he had caused to be reserved. On principle Jeannie felt bound to remonstrate.

"You are so extravagant," she said. "I know exactly what that means: you have paid for four places."

"Three," he said. "You have paid for your own. And if you say a word more I shall get another compartment for your maid."

Jeannie laughed.

"My lips are dumb," she said. "Ah! it is good to see you."

She was for the moment deprived of that particular blessing, for he went out again to get a tea-basket, and Jeannie leant back in her seat, feeling, in spite of her remonstrance, that exquisite pleasure that comes from being looked after, from having everything done for you, not from a man's mere politeness, but from his right (he, the one man) to serve the one woman. In all he did he was so intensely efficient and reliable; the most casual trivial detail, if entrusted to him, took place as by some immutable natural law. He would return in the shortest possible time, yet without hurry, with the tea-basket, while half that crowd of jostling, distracted passengers outside would have to go without. And it was not otherwise in things that were far from trivial. When he told her he loved her she knew that she stood on an unshakable rock, against which nothing could prevail. There was not a woman in the world, she felt, as safe as she. Well she knew what lay beneath his quietness and undemonstrativeness, a trust how complete, a love how strong.

The train started, then he leant forward to her from his seat opposite and took both her hands.

"My dearest," he said, and kissed her.

And then there was silence for a little.

"And your plans," he said at last—"your immediate plans, I mean? You go to Lady Nottingham's in town now, don't you?"

"Yes; and you? Will you be in town?"

A smile just smouldered in his eyes.

"Well, just possibly," he said. "I hope we may meet now and then. She has asked me down to Bray the day after to-morrow for Whitsuntide. Shall I go?"

Jeannie laughed.

"I won't pretend not to know what that means," she said. "It means to ask whether I am going. What shall we do? I suppose the house will be full, whereas we might have a sort of dear little desert island all to ourselves if we stopped in town, as everybody will be away. I should not object to that in the least. But, Victor, if Alice wants me, I think I had better go down with her. There aren't really any people in the world except you and me, but they think there are." Her brown eyes softened again. "I think that is an ungrateful and selfish speech of mine," she said. "I am sorry; I don't deserve my friends."

"I like the ungrateful and selfish speech," said he.

"Then I present you with it. Yes, I think we had better go down there. I long to see Alice again, and Daisy. Dear Daisy, have you seen her lately?"

"As one may say that one has seen a meteor. She has flashed by."

"Ah, Daisy shall not flash by me. She must flash to me, and stop there, burning. Oh, look, it is the month of the briar-rose. See how the hedges foam with pink blossom. And the fields, look, knee-deep in long grasses and daisies and buttercups. I am home again, thank Heaven. I am home. Home met me on the pier, my darling—the heart of home met me there."

"And you did not expect it in the least?" he asked. "You said so, at any rate."

"Did I really? What very odd things one says! It is lucky that nobody believes them."

CHAPTER IV.

They parted at Victoria, and Mrs. Halton drove straight to Lady Nottingham's, leaving her maid to claim and capture her luggage. She had not known till she returned to London how true a Londoner she was at heart, how closely the feel and sense of the great grey dirty city was knit into her self. For it was the soil out of which had grown all the things in her life which "counted" or were significant; it had been the scene of all her great joys and sorrows, and to-day all those who made up her intimate life, friends and lover, were gathered here.

There were many other places in the world to which she felt grateful: sunny hillsides overlooking the spires of Florence; cool woods on the Italian Riviera through which stirred the fresh breezes off the dim blue sea below; galleries and churches of Venice, and the grey-green stretches of its lagoons. To all these her debt of gratitude was deep, for it was in them, and through their kindly sunny aid, that during the last year she had recaptured peace and content.

But her gratitude to them was not of the quality of love; she felt rather towards them as a patient feels towards the doctors and nurses to whose ministrations he owes his return of health and the removal of the fever which, while it lasted, came between himself and the whole world, making all things strange and unreal. And then, just for a moment, a little shudder passed over her as she thought of the sharp-edged, shining streets of Paris through which she had passed with downcast, averted eyes that morning, going straight from station to station and hating every moment of her passage.

It was hard to forgive Paris for associations which it held for her of a certain fortnight; it was hard to believe even now that those bitter and miserable hours contained no more than the pain by which it was necessary that a dear and erring soul should be taught its lessons. But at heart she did not doubt that, though she could not forgive Paris for being the scene of those infinitely sad and pitiful memories. Then she shook those thoughts off; they concerned that past which was absolutely dead in so far as it was painful and bitter, and lived only in the greater tenderness and pity of which her own soul was so full.

There was an affectionate little note of greeting and welcome for her from Lady Nottingham, which was at once given her, and even as she read it somewhere overhead a door opened, and like a whirlwind Daisy descended.

"Oh, Aunt Jeannie," she cried, "how heavenly! Oh, it is quite good enough to be true. You darling person! I have never liked anything nearly as much as this minute."

Daisy made a sort of Bacchante of herself as she took her aunt up to the drawing-room, dancing round her, and ever and again rushing in upon her for another kiss.

"And I managed everything too beautifully," she said. "Aunt Alice wasn't sure if she wouldn't put off an engagement in order to be here when you arrived, and I said she oughtn't to. I put it on moral grounds, and packed her and Gladys off. And I didn't care half a row of pins for moral grounds, I only just wanted to get the first half-hour with you all to myself. And if you aren't pleased at my plan I shall burst into several tears."

Aunt Jeannie took the dear face between her hands.

"I couldn't have thought of a better plan myself," she said, "and, as you know, I am rather proud of my plans when I really give my mind to them. Oh, Daisy, it *is* good to see you! I don't think a day has passed without my just longing to have a glimpse at you."

"Oh, is that all?" said Daisy. "I know a day hasn't passed without my longing to have many glimpses."

"You dear child! You shall have such a lot. And what a lot you will have to tell me; I shall want to know exactly what you have done, and whether you've been wise and good and kind, and what new friends you have. I shall want to see them all, and make friends with them all. And I shall want to know all your plans. Just think, Daisy, it's a year since I saw you."

"I know, but I don't believe it. Oh, Aunt Jeannie, you must come down to Bray for Whitsuntide. Gladys and I go to-morrow just to look round and see that everything is all right, and you and Aunt Alice are to come the next day with all the party, and it will be such fun. Oh! I've got such a lot to tell you."

Daisy paused a moment.

"I think I mean quite the opposite," she said. "I don't think that I've anything whatever to tell you that's of the very smallest importance. I only just want to babble and be glad. I am glad, oh, so frightfully glad! You are the nicest aunt that anybody ever had."

Daisy poured out tea for her aunt, and considering her admission that she had nothing to say, made a very substantial job of it. Yet all the time she was talking with a reservation, having clearly made up her mind not to mention Lord Lindfield's name. She felt sure, if she did,

Aunt Jeannie would see that she mentioned him somehow differently from the way in which she mentioned others, and these first moments of meeting, for all the sincerity of her joy to see her, struck her as not suitable for confidences.

"Another reason why I wanted half an hour with you," she said, "is that I am dining out to-night, and shan't see you. It is quite too disgusting, but I couldn't help myself; and if one dines out one probably dances, you know, so after this I shan't see you at all till to-morrow. Oh, Aunt Jeannie, what a nice world it is! I am glad I happened to be born. And you are looking so young, I can't think why everybody doesn't want to marry you at once. They probably do."

Mrs. Halton's engagement was at present a secret, for it was still only just a year since her husband's death, and though that had been a release merciful both to him and her, her wisdom had rightly decided that the event should not be announced yet. They were to be married in the autumn, and the news need not be made public immediately. One reservation she had made, namely, that she would tell Lady Nottingham; but Daisy, even Daisy, must not know at present.

She laughed.

"They have a remarkable power of keeping their desires to themselves, then," she said. "Dover pier"—and she smiled inwardly as she said it—"was not thick with aspirants for my rather large hand. But as we are on the subject, Daisy, what about Mr. Carton?"

Daisy looked at her imploringly.

"Oh, don't!" she said. "There is nothing more to tell you than what I have written to you. He's so much too good for me that I should feel uncomfortably inferior, which is never pleasant. Oh, Aunt Jeannie, what a fraud I am! That isn't the reason a bit—and the reason is simply that I don't want to. It sounds so easy to understand, doesn't it, when it's stated like that, but poor darling Willie finds it so difficult to grasp. I had to say it all over again three times last Monday. It isn't that I feel inferior to him. If I did, it might mean that I was in love with him, because people always say that they aren't the least worthy when they fully intend to marry each other. No. I don't want to, that's all; and if I am to be an old maid with a canary—well, I shall be an old maid with a canary, which I shall instantly sell, because they make such a row, don't they? Do you think we might talk about something else?"

It was scarcely necessary for Daisy to add the last sentence, for without pause she proceeded to do so. At the back of her mind Mrs. Halton felt that there was something behind this, but since Daisy clearly did not desire to speak of it, she would be committing the crime—almost unpardonable between friends—of attempting to force a confidence, if she showed the slightest eagerness to hear more or even let her manner betray that she thought there was more to be heard. Besides, she had her own secret from Daisy. It would be a meanness to deny to others the liberty she claimed herself.

Lady Nottingham came in soon after this, and before long the two girls had to go and dress for their dinner. Daisy, in the highest spirits, rushed in again to say good-night to the aunts before starting, a ravishing figure.

"Good-night, darling Aunt Jeannie," she cried. "Yes, my frock is nice, isn't it?—and it cost twopence-halfpenny! Wasn't it a cheap shop? Silver has gone down in value, you see, so much, and green was always cheap. It's too heavenly to think that I shall come back to the house where you are. Usually I hate coming back from balls."

A cab was waiting for them, and Daisy pulled the window down with a jerk.

"She's a darling!" she exclaimed, "and I want to tell her everything, Gladys, yet not one word did I say about Lord Lindfield. I have a perfectly good reason as to why I did not in my own mind, but it doesn't happen to be the right one. I say to myself that I wish to tell her nothing until there is really something to tell. But that isn't the real reason. Do you generally have a good reason *and* a real reason? I always do. Then you can use either and satisfy anybody. I think I must be a hypocrite. The real reason is that I think she would see that I wasn't in love with him. Well, I'm not—but I'm going to be. I shall tell her then."

"Is he going to be at the Streathams to-night?" asked Gladys.

"Yes, of course. That's why I am going. If he wasn't, I should say I was ill, and stop at home with Aunt Jeannie. Darling, if you look shocked I shall be sick! Every girl wants to see the man she intends to marry as often as possible. But most girls don't say so; that is why, as a sex, we are such unutterable humbugs. Men are so much more sensible. They say, 'She's a ripper!' or 'a clipper!'—or whatever is the word in use—'and I shall go and call on that cad of a woman with whom she is dining on Thursday next, in order to be asked to dinner.' That's sensible; there's no nonsense about it. But girls pretend it happens by accident. As if anything happened by accident! They plot and scheme in just the same way, only they aren't frank about it. We want to marry certain men just as much as they want to marry us, and yet we pretend they do it all. You pretend. You try to look shocked because I don't. Here we are! Oh, do get out! No, you needn't hurry. He's coming up the pavement now. If you get out quick he won't see us—me, I mean!"

This slogging diplomacy was successful. Lord Lindfield got opposite the house exactly as Daisy stepped out of the cab.

"Hullo, Miss Daisy!" he said. "What stupendous luck! Thought I was going into the wilderness to-night like the children of Israel—and here you are! Jove!"

He had taken off his hat, and stood bare-headed as he handed her out of the cab, exposing that fascinating greyness above the temples which Daisy had spoken of. A face clean-shaven and so bubblingly good-humoured that all criticism of his features was futile appeared below, but a reader of character might easily guess that if once that bubbling good-humour were expunged, something rather serious and awkward might be left. But the good-humour seemed ineradicable; no one could picture his face without it. In other respects, he was very broad, but of sufficient height to carry off the breadth without giving the appearance of being short. A broken front tooth, often exposed by laughter, completed the general irregularity of his face. The fascinating greyness was accompanied by a tendency to high forehead, due probably to incipient baldness rather than to abnormal intellectual development.

"I don't know what Jove has got to do with it," said Daisy; "but if he is responsible, I think it is delightful of him. I am glad you are here. I thought I was going into the wilderness too. Oh, I think you have met my cousin."

He had met Gladys about a hundred times, so Daisy was quite right, and they shook hands gravely. That ceremony over, he turned to Daisy again without pause.

"Dance, too, isn't there?" he said. "I shan't know a soul. I never do. Do dance with me sometimes, out of pity's sake, Miss Daisy—just now and then, you know."

Daisy gave an altogether excessive florin to the cabman, who held it in the palm of his hand, and looked at it as if it were some curious botanical specimen hitherto unknown to him.

"And one usually says 'Thank you!'" she observed.— "Yes, Lord Lindfield, let's dance now and then."

CHAPTER V.

Their dancing now and then chiefly assumed the less violent form of dancing, namely, sitting in as sequestered places as they could find. There was nothing very sequestered, as the house was rather small and the guests extremely numerous, and they sat generally in full view of the whole world, Daisy being occasionally torn away by other partners and being annexed again by him on the earliest possible occasion. In such absences, though the good-humour of his face showed no sign of abatement, he became extremely distrait, failed to recognize people he knew quite well, and took up his stand firmly at the door of the ballroom, where he could observe her and be at hand as soon as she was disengaged again.

Their hostess, Mrs. Streatham, was a very rich and gloriously pushing woman, with no nonsense about her, and but little sense. She was engaged in pushing her way steadily upwards through what is known as the top-crust of society, and if she wanted anybody particularly to come to her house, gave him or her the choice of some six dinners and ten lunches, further facilitating matters by requesting the desired object to drop in any time. It was Lord Lindfield's first appearance at her house, and she was already pinning him down for a further lunch some time next week, with a grim tenacity of purpose that made it difficult to evade her. He did not propose to leave his post of observation at the ballroom door till this dance came to an end; and as she had as good a right there (since it was her own house) as he, it was likely that she would get her way. He had begun—which was a tactical error—by saying he was not free till the end of the week, and this gave her an advantage. She gave her invitation in a calm, decided manner—rather in the manner of a dentist making appointments.

"Thursday, Friday, or Saturday will suit me equally well, Lord Lindfield," she was saying. "I shall have a few people to lunch on all those days, and you can take your choice. Shall we say Friday?"

"It's awfully kind of you," said he, "but I'm really not quite sure about Friday. I rather think I'm already engaged."

"Saturday, then," said Mrs. Streatham, "at one-thirty."

"Very kind of you, but I'm away for the week-end, and shall probably have to leave town in the morning."

"Then let us make it Thursday," said Mrs. Streatham. "And if two o'clock suits you better than half-past one, it is equally convenient. That will be delightful."

At the moment the dance came to an end, and Lindfield, to his dismay, saw Daisy leaving by a further door.

"Very good of you," he said. "I'll be sure to remember. Excuse me."

Mrs. Streatham was quite ready to excuse him now, since she had her hook in him, and went on to Gladys, who was just passing out.

"Miss Hinton," she said, "do lunch with me on Thursday next. Lord Lindfield is coming, and, I hope, a few more friends. Or Friday would suit me equally well. I hope Miss Hanbury will come too. Would you ask her?—or perhaps it is safer that I should send her a note. Thursday, then, at two.—Ah! Lord Quantock, I have been looking for you all evening. Pray lunch here on Thursday next. Lord Lindfield and Miss Hinton, and that very pretty Daisy—let me see, what is her name?— oh, yes!—Daisy Hanbury are coming. Or, if you are engaged that day, do drop in on Friday at the same time."

Lord Lindfield meantime had found Daisy and firmly taken her away from her partner. Before now, as has been said, the affair was a matter of common discussion, and her engagement believed to be only a matter of time; to-night it looked as if the time would be short.

"And I'm coming down to Bray this week-end," he said, going on at the point at which their conversation was interrupted. "It was so good of Lady Nottingham to ask me. You've got such nice aunts! I expect that accounts for a lot in you. Ever seen my aunts, Miss Daisy? They've got whiskers, and take camomile."

"It sounds delicious, and I'm sure I should love them," said Daisy.—"So sorry, Mr. Tracy, but I seem to have made a mistake, and I'm engaged for the next. So very stupid of me.—I know, Lord Lindfield; isn't Aunt Alice a darling? But, although I adore her, I think I adore Aunt Jeannie more. Do you know her—Mrs. Halton?"

Lindfield gave a little appreciative whistle.

"Know her? By Jove! I should think I did. So she's your aunt, too! I never heard such luck! But she's a bit young to be an aunt, isn't she?"

Daisy laughed.

"She began early. She was my mother's sister, but ever so much younger. She was an aunt when she was eight. My eldest sister, you know——"

"Didn't know you had one."

"Very likely you wouldn't. She died some years ago, and before that she didn't live in England. She was married to a Frenchman. But Aunt Jeannie—isn't she an angel? And she came back from Italy, where she has been for a whole year, only to-day. It's the nicest thing that has happened since she went away."

"You mean that was nice?"

"Oh, don't be so silly! It is quite clear what I mean. You'll see her next week; she is coming down to Bray."

"Wonder if she'll remember me? The people I like most hardly ever do. Rather sad! I say, Miss Daisy, I'm looking forward to that visit to Bray like anything. I don't know when I've looked forward to anything so much. Are you good at guessing? I wonder if you can guess why?"

The room where they sat had somewhat emptied of its tenants, since the next dance had just begun, and something in his tone, some sudden tremble of his rather deep voice, some brightness in those merry grey eyes, suddenly struck Daisy, and just for the moment it frightened her. She put all her gaiety and lightness into her reply.

"Ah, but clearly," she said, "it is quite easy to guess. It is because you will see Aunt Jeannie again. You have told me as much."

"Not quite right," he said, "but pretty near. Bother! Here's that woman coming to ask me to lunch again."

The good humour quite vanished from his face as Mrs. Streatham came rapidly towards them. She had so much to think about with all her invitations that she very seldom remembered to smile. And it was without a smile that she bore rapidly down upon them.

"Oh, Miss—Miss Hanbury," she said, "do come to lunch on Thursday next at one-thirty—or is it two, Lord Lindfield? Yes, two. Lord Lindfield is coming, and I hope one or two other friends."

"Why, that is charming of you," said Daisy. "I shall be delighted."

"And do persuade Lady Nottingham to come, will you not?" continued Mrs. Streatham. "She is your aunt, is she not?"

Somehow the moment had passed, but Daisy, as she stood talking, felt that something new had come to her. She had seen Tom Lindfield for a moment in a new light: for that second she felt that she had never known him before. He struck her differently, somehow, and it was that which momentarily had frightened her, and caused her to make that light, nonsensical reply. But next moment she saw that it was not he who had altered, it was herself.

All this was very faint and undefined in her own mind. But it was there.

CHAPTER VI.

Jeannie Halton, going up to her bedroom that night, felt very keenly that ineffable sense of coming home which makes all the hours spent in alien places seem dim and unreal. She could hardly believe that it was she who had been so long away from so many friends, still less that it was she who, a year ago, tired and weary, had gone southwards in search of that minimum of health and peace which makes existence tolerable. Yet that time abroad could never have become dim to her, since it was there, in the winter spent in Rome, that her old friendship with Victor Braithwaite had ripened into intimacy and burst into love. Rome would always be knit into her life.

It was not only in affairs of the mind and affections that her perception was acute. Like most highly-organized people, her body, her fine material senses, were vivid messengers to her soul; and as she went upstairs she contrasted with a strong sense of content her purely physical surroundings with those in which she had lived for the last forty-eight hours. For two days and nights she had been hurried across Europe, over the jolt and rattle of the racing wheels; by day the blurred landscape, wreathed in engine-smoke, had streamed by her; by night she had seen nothing but the dull, stuffed walls of her sleeping compartment, and it was an exquisite physical pleasure to have the firm, unshaken floor underfoot, to be surrounded by the appointments of a beautiful house, to be able to move of one's own volition again, and not to be taken like a parcel in a van from one end of Europe to the other. And how delicious also it was to be clean, to have revelled in soap and water, instead of being coated and pelted at by dust and coal-grime! On the surface of life this was all pleasant; it all added to her sense of security and well-being.

She had enjoyed a charming evening, which was not nearly over yet, since Alice was coming to her room for a talk—no little talk, no few good-night words, but a real long talk, which should wipe off the arrears of a twelve months' abstinence. Alice had demurred at first, saying she knew that journeys were fatiguing things, but Mrs. Halton had truthfully said that she had never felt less tired. For when one is happy there is no time to be fatigued; being happy engrosses the whole attention. It was early yet also, scarcely after ten, for two or three old friends only, a party of women, had dined, and these had gone away early, with the fatigue of the traveller in their minds. Mrs. Halton had let that pass; the fact was that to-night she wanted above all things to talk to Lady Nottingham. There was one thing—a very big one—

which she meant to tell her, and there was also a great deal she wished to learn.

Lady Nottingham followed her after a minute or two; and a maid bearing a tray with an enormous jug of hot water and a glass followed Lady Nottingham, for she was one of those people who seem to keep permanently young by always doing the latest thing. Just now there was a revival of hot-water drinking, and with avidity (as if it tasted nice) Lady Nottingham drank hot water.

"Excellent thing, Jeannie," she said. "Can't I persuade you to try? You dear person, I don't know that I will even attempt to. It might have some effect on you, and I don't want anything to have any effect on you. I prefer you exactly as you are. Now I want to make myself quite comfortable, in order that I may enjoy myself as much as possible, and then you shall tell me all that has happened to you this last year.—No, Hendon, you needn't wait up. Yes; plenty of hot water. Go to bed."

"Let me pull the blinds up and open the windows," said Jeannie; "I want to let London in. Ah! Clip-clop! Clip-clop! Girls and boys going to dances, and falling in love with one another, and keeping the world young. God bless them!"

She leant out into the soft warm night a moment, and then turned back into the room again, her face so brimming with happiness and youth that Alice for a moment was almost startled.

"They or something else seems to have kept you young, you dear!" she said. "And now sit down and tell me all about yourself from the crown of your head to the sole of your foot. You are so tall, too, Jeannie; it will take a nice long time."

Jeannie sat down.

"So it is 'me next,' is it, as the children say?" she asked. "Very well, me. Well, once upon a time, dear, a year ago, I was an old woman. I was twenty-nine, if you care to know, but an old woman. For the measure of years is a very bad standard to judge by; it tells you of years only which have practically nothing to do with being old or young. Well, the old woman of twenty-nine went away. And to-day she came back, a year older in respect of years, since she is thirty now, but, oh! ever so much younger, because—— Do you guess at all?"

Lady Nottingham put down her hot water.

"Ah! my dear," she said, "of course I guess. Or rather I don't guess; I know. There is somebody. It is only

Somebody who can interfere in our age and our happiness. Who is it?"

"No; guess again," said Jeannie.

But again it was hardly a case of guessing. Lady Nottingham knew quite well who it was, who in those years of Jeannie's married life had been her constant and quiet support and stand-by, and who had found his reward in the knowledge that he helped her to bear what had to be borne.

"Victor Braithwaite," she said, without pause. "Oh, Jeannie, is it so? You are going to marry him? Oh, my darling, I am so glad. What a happy man, and how well he deserves it!"

Lady Nottingham was stout and comfortable; but with extraordinary alertness she surged out of her chair to kiss Jeannie, and upset the table on which was her glass and her boiling water, breaking the one and deluging the carpet with the other—a perfect Niagara of scalding fluid. She paid not the least attention to the rising clouds of steam nor to the glass which crashed on to the floor and was reduced to shards and exploded fragments.

"My dear, how nice!" she said. "And he has been in love with you so long! He will have told you that now, but I insist on the credit of having seen it also. He behaved so splendidly, and was such a good friend to you, without ever letting you see—for I will wager that you did not—that he loved you."

"No, I never knew until he told me," said Jeannie, simply.

"Of course you didn't, because he is a nice man and you are a nice woman. Oh, Jeannie, don't you hate those creatures who keep a man dangling—wives, I mean—who like knowing that a man is eating his poor silly heart out for them, who don't intend to lead—well, double lives, and yet keep him tied to their apron-strings? Such vampires! They put their dreadful noses in the air the moment he says something to them that he shouldn't, and all the time they have been encouraging him to say it! They are flirts, who will certainly find themselves in a very uncomfortable round of the Inferno! I should torture them if I were Providence! I am sure Providence would prefer—— Dear me, yes."

Alice kissed her again.

"Isn't it so?" she demanded, vehemently.

"About flirts? Why, of course. A flirt is a woman who leads a man on and leads him on, and then suddenly says, 'What do you mean?' Surely we need not discuss them."

Lady Nottingham went over to the window-seat.

"No, I know we need not," she said. "I was led away. Darling, Victor Braithwaite is coming to Bray on Saturday. Did you ever hear of anything more apt? Till this moment I was not sure that you would ever marry him, though I longed for you to do so. You shall have a punt all to yourselves—a private particular punt—and he shall—well, he shall punt you about. Oh, Jeannie, I too love the youth of the world."

Jeannie drew her chair a little nearer to the window-seat, in which Lady Nottingham had taken her place after the catastrophe of the hot water.

"I know. He told me he was coming to Bray to-day."

"Oh, he met you at Victoria?" she asked.

"No, dear; a little further down the line—at Dover, in fact. Yes, Alice, his was the first face I saw as we came alongside. And how my heart went out to him! What a good homecoming it has been, and how absolutely unworthy I feel of it! You have no idea how I used to rebel and complain in—in those past years, wondering what I had done to have my life so spoilt. Spoilt! Yes, that was the word I used to myself, and all the time this was coming nearer."

"Tell me more, dear."

"About him?" asked Jeannie.

"About him and you."

"Well, all the autumn I was on the Italian lakes. Oh, Alice, such dreadful months, and all the more dreadful because of the maddening beauty of the place. I looked at it. I knew it was all there, but I never saw it; it never went inside me, or went to make part of me. I was very sleepless all that time, and depressed with a blackness of despair. And as I got stronger in physical health, the depression seemed more unbearable, because, in all probability, so many years lay before me, and nothing in life seemed the least worth while. I often thought of you, and often—every day—of Daisy, longing, in a way, to see you both, but knowing that it would be no use if I did, for you would have been to me like the corpses, the husks of what I loved once. And I did not see any possibility of getting better or of getting out of this tomb-like darkness. It was like being buried alive, and getting more alive from week to week, so that I grew more and more conscious of how black the tomb was. Every now and then the pall used to lift a little, and that, I think, was the worst of all."

Lady Nottingham laid her plump, comfortable hand on Jeannie's.

"You poor darling!" she said. "And you would not let either Daisy or me come to you. Why did you not?"

"Because there are certain passages, I think, which the human soul has to go through alone. Dear Alice, you don't know all that went to make up the gloom of those dreadful months! There was one thing in particular that cast a blacker shadow than all the rest. I hope you will never know it. It concerns some one who is dead, but not my husband. It was that which made the darkness so impenetrable. I know you will not ask me about it. But, as I said, when the pall lifted a little, that was the worst of all, because then, for a moment it might be, or for an hour or two, I knew that life and youth and joy were just as dominant and as triumphant as ever in the world, and that it was I who had got on the wrong side of things, and saw them left-handed, and could be only conscious of this hideous nightmare of suffering."

Jeannie paused again, pushing back the thick coils of black hair from her forehead.

"Quite little things would make the pall lift," she said. "Once it was the sudden light of the sun shining on one of those red sails; once it was the sight of a little Italian contadina dancing with her shadow on the white sunny road, all by herself, for sheer exuberance of heart; once it was a man and a maid sitting close to each other in the dusk, and quietly singing some little love-song, so—so dreadfully unconscious of the sorrow of the world. Oh, that was bad—that was dreadful! Just one little verse, and then in the darkness they kissed each other. I knew they were darlings, and I thought they were devils. And once Victor wrote to me, saying that he was passing through on his way to Venice and Rome, and asking if he might come to see me. I did not answer him even; I could not.

"But during all those weeks I suppose I was getting better, and when I went south to Rome in November, though I still could not look forward or contemplate the future at all, I knew better how to deal with the present hour and the present day. There was no joy in them, but there was a sort of acquiescence in me. If life—as seemed the only possible thing—was to be joyless for me, I could at least behave decently. Also a certain sort of pride, I think, came to my help. I felt that it was bad manners to appear as I felt—just as when one has a headache one makes an effort to appear more brilliantly well than usual. One doesn't like people to know one has a headache, and in the same way I settled that I didn't like them to know I had a heartache.

"Victor was in Rome. The manager of the branch of their banking business there had died suddenly, and he had gone to take his place till some one could be sent out from England. The new man arrived there some ten days or so after I did; but he still stayed on, for one morning I saw him in the Forum, and another day I passed him driving. All he knew was that I had not answered the letter which he wrote to me when I was on Como, and he made no further attempt to see me. But he did not leave Rome. And then one day I wrote to him, as I was bound to do, saying that I had not answered his letter because I believed then that I could not; but that if he would forgive that, and come to see me——

"Oh, Alice, it is being such a long story. But there is little more. He came, and I asked him if he was stopping long in Rome, and he said his plans were uncertain. And then—so gradually that I scarcely knew it was happening—he began to take care of me; and gradually, also, I began to expect him to do so. He tells me I was not tiresome; I can't believe him.

"And then—how does it happen? Nobody knows, though it has happened so often. One day I saw him differently. I had always been friends with him, and in those bad years I had always relied on him; but, as I say, one day I saw him differently. I saw the man himself—not as he struck me, but as he was. That is just it, dear Alice. 'How he struck me' was left out, because I was left out. And then I knew I loved him. And—and that is all, I think."

Lady Nottingham gave a long, appreciative sigh.

"I think it is *the* nicest story," she said—"and it's all true. Oh, Jeannie, I am such a match-maker, and it is so pleasant to be forestalled. I asked him down to Bray simply in order to promote this, and now I find it has been promoted already. But the punt will be useful all the same."

Jeannie joined her friend in the window-seat.

"Yes, just the same," she said.

CHAPTER VII.

There was silence for a little while. An hour had passed since they began to talk, but it was still short of midnight, and the hansoms and motors still swept about the square like a throng of sonorous fireflies. Just opposite a big house flared with lit windows, and the sound of the band came loudly across the open space, a little mellowed by the distance, but with the rhythm of its music intact.

"Oh, I could get into a ball-dress and go and dance now for lightness of heart," said Jeannie. "But I won't; I will do something much nicer, and that is I will hear from you the news of your year. Now it is 'you next.' Tell me all you have done and been and thought of. And then I shall want to know all about Gladys and all about Daisy. I talked to Daisy—or, rather, she talked to me—for half an hour this afternoon, but I don't think she got absolutely 'home' in her talk. I had the impression that she was showing me the dining-room and drawing-room, so to speak. She did not sit with me in my bedroom or in hers as we are sitting now. The only talk worth calling a talk is when you put your feet on the fender and tuck up your skirt and put the lights out—figuratively, that is. One must be taken into privacy. Daisy wasn't very private. You have got to be. Now, dear Alice, about yourself first."

Alice sighed again—not appreciatively this time.

"There's very little to say. I am rather lazier than I was, and Daisy and Gladys—Daisy chiefly—make all arrangements. I send them out to dances alone, because they always find a chaperon of some kind; and you know, Jeannie, I don't like hot rooms and supper. I weave plenty of plans still, and they mostly come off, but I don't go to superintend the execution of them. I don't think I have any very private life; if I had you should at once be admitted. I think a great deal about the people I like best. I try occasionally to straighten out their affairs for them. I want all girls to marry suitable men, and all men to marry suitable girls. I think, indeed, that the only change in me has been that I take a rather wider view than I used to of the word suitable. You see, I am an optimist, and I can't help it; and I believe that most people are kind and nice. Oh, I don't say that it is not great fun being critical and seeing their absurdities and their faults, but I fancy that if one wants to increase the sum of comfort and happiness in the world, it is better to spend one's time in trying to see their charms and their virtues. Dear me, what dreadful commonplaces I am saying! However, that is my very truthful history for the last year: I want to make people jolly and comfortable and happy, but, if possible, without standing about in extremely hot rooms with the band playing into one's ear at the distance of three inches."

Jeannie laughed.

"I don't think that is at all a bad history," she said. "That is just the sort of history which I hope will be written of me by-and-by. Oh, Alice, I don't want any more troubles and crises—I don't! I don't!—even if they are good for one. Sometimes I wonder if there is some envious power that is always on the look-out, some Nemesis with a dreadful wooden eye that waits till we are happy and then puts out a great bony hand and knocks us over or squeezes us till we scream. 'Oh, Nemesis,' I feel inclined to say, 'do look the other way for a little bit.' Yes, I just want Nemesis to leave my friends and me alone for a little."

"Ah! but Nemesis is looking the other way with great fixedness, it seems to me," said Lady Nottingham. "She may be dabbing away at other people, but you must be just, Jeannie; she hasn't been dabbing at any of us lately."

"Oh, hush! Don't say it so loud," said Jeannie. "She may hear and turn round."

Alice laughed.

"No such thing," she said. "But Nemesis will certainly send you a headache and a feeling of being tired to-morrow morning if I sit up talking to you any longer."

She half rose, but Jeannie pulled her back into the window-seat again.

"Oh, no; don't go yet," she said. "I am not the least tired, and it is so dull going to bed. I hoard pleasant hours; I make them last as long as possible, and surely we can lengthen out this one for a little more. Besides, you have not told me one word about Daisy yet; and, as I said, though I had half an hour's talk with her, I feel as if she hadn't taken me into her room. All the private history she gave me was that Willie Carton still wanted to marry her, and she still did not want to marry him."

Lady Nottingham considered this for a moment in silence, wondering whether, as Daisy had not spoken to her aunt about Lord Lindfield, she herself was under any tacit bond of secrecy. But, scrupulous though she was, she could not see any cause for secrecy.

Jeannie interrupted her silence.

"Is there somebody else?" she said.

Again Lady Nottingham thought over it.

"I can't see why I shouldn't tell you," she said, "since half London knows, and is waiting quite sympathetically and agreeably for him to ask her. She consulted me about it only this afternoon, and I think when he does—I don't say if, because I feel sure he will—I think that when he does she will accept him. I advised her to, and I think she agreed. His name——"

"Ah, but perhaps Daisy wants to tell me his name herself," interrupted Jeannie again. "Perhaps she wants to keep it as a surprise for me. Don't tell me his name, Alice. Tell me all about him, though not enough to enable me to guess. And tell me about Daisy's feelings towards him. Somehow I don't think a girl should need advice; she should know for herself, don't you think?"

"Not always. Sometimes, of course, a girl is definitely, even desperately, in love with a man before she marries—but, Jeannie, how often it is the other way! She likes him, she thinks he will be kind to her, she wants to be married, she has all the reasons for marrying except that of being in love. And such marriages so often turn out so well; some even turn out ideally. My own did. But in some circumstances I think a girl is right to ask advice."

Jeannie smiled.

"I think yours is an admirably sensible view, dear," she said, "and I confess freely that there is heaps to be said for it. But I am afraid I am not sensible over a thing like love. I think sense ought to be banished."

"So do the lower classes think," remarked Lady Nottingham, rather acutely, "and the consequence is that the gravest problem that has ever faced the nation has arisen."

"Oh, I take it, he is not one of the unemployed?" said Jeannie.

"He is, but the top end of them."

"Oh, go on, dear; tell me all about him," said Jeannie.

"Well, he is rich—I suppose you might say very rich—he has a title; he has an old and honoured name."

"Oh, I want something more important than all that," said Jeannie. "The old and honoured name is all very well, but is he continuing to make it honoured? To be honoured yourself is far more to the point than having centuries full of honoured ancestors. Is he satisfactory? I can easily forgive the ancestors for being unsatisfactory."

"I am sure he is a good fellow," said Lady Nottingham.

Jeannie got up and began walking up and down the room.

"Do you know, that is such an ambiguous phrase!" she said. "Every man is a good fellow who eats a lot and laughs a lot and flirts a lot. Is he that sort of good fellow? Oh! I hate milksops. I needn't tell you that; but there are plenty of good fellows whom I should be sorry to see Daisy married to."

There had started up in Jeannie's mind that memory of Paris, which had made her hurry through and away from the town; there had started up in her mind also that which had been so hard to get over in the autumn, that of which she had spoken to Alice Nottingham, only to tell her that she hoped she would never speak of it. These two were connected. They were more than connected, for they were the same; and now a fear, fantastic, perhaps, but definite, grew in her mind that once again these things were to be made vivid, to pass into currency.

"Is he that sort of good fellow?" she asked.

There was trouble in her voice and anxiety, and Lady Nottingham was startled. It was as if some ghost had come into the room, visible to Jeannie. But her answer could not be put off or postponed.

"Something troubles you, dear," she said. "I can't guess what. Yes, he is that sort of good fellow, I suppose; but don't you think you generalize too much, when you class them all together? And don't you judge harshly? Cannot a man have—to use the cant phrase—have sown his wild oats, and have done with them? Mind, I know nothing definite about those wild oats, but before now it has been a matter of gossip that he has been very—very susceptible, and that women find him charming. It is disgusting, no doubt. But I fully believe he has done with such things. Is he not to have his chance in winning a girl like Daisy, and becoming a model husband and father? Don't you judge harshly?"

Jeannie paused in her walk opposite her friend, and stood looking out into the warm, soft night.

"Yes, perhaps I judge harshly," she said, "because I know what awful harm a man of that sort can do. I am thinking of what a man of that sort did do. He was no worse than others, I daresay, and he was most emphatically a good fellow. But the woman concerned in it all was one I knew and loved, and so I can't forgive him or his kind. You and I have both known lots of men of the kind, have found them agreeable and well-bred and all the rest of it; and, without doubt, many of them settle down and become model husbands and model fathers. But I am sorry—I am sorry. If only Daisy had cared for Willie Carton! And she does not love this man, you say?"

"He attracts and interests her; she finds great pleasure in his company; she wants to marry him. I am not what you would call a worldly woman, Jeannie, but I think she is wise. It is an excellent match, and in spite of what you say about so-called 'good fellows,' he is a good fellow."

Jeannie's face had grown suddenly rather white and tired. She felt as if Nemesis were slowly turning round in her direction again. She sat down by her dressing-table and drummed her fingers on it.

"Yes, no doubt I judge harshly," she repeated, "and no doubt, also, there is a particular fear in my brain, quite fantastic probably and quite without foundation. I have a 'good fellow' in my mind whose—whose 'good-fellow proceedings' touched me very acutely. I want, therefore, to know the name of this man. I can't help it; if Daisy wants it to be a surprise for me, she must be disappointed. You see what my fear is, that the two are the same. So tell me his name, Alice."

There was something so desperately serious in her tone that Lady Nottingham did not think of reassuring her out of her fears, but answered at once.

"Lord Lindfield," she said.

The drumming of Jeannie's fingers on the table ceased. She sat quite still, looking out in front of her.

"Lord Lindfield?" she asked. "Tom Lindfield?"

"Yes."

Jeannie got up.

"Then thank Heaven she doesn't love him," she said. "It is quite impossible that she should marry him. Since you began to tell me about this man I was afraid it was Tom Lindfield, hoping, hoping desperately, that it was not. She can never marry him, never—never! What are we to do? What are we to do?"

"There is some reason behind this, then, that I don't know?" asked Alice.

"Of course there is. I must tell you, I suppose. We must put our heads together and plan and plan. Oh, Alice, I hoped so much for peace and happiness, but it can't be yet, not until we have settled this."

"But what is it? What is it?" asked Lady Nottingham.

A hansom jingled round the corner and stopped just below at the front door.

"The girls are back," said Jeannie. "Daisy is sure to come and see if I am up. I wonder why they are home so early. You must go, dear Alice. I will tell you about it to-morrow. I am so tired, so suddenly and frightfully tired."

Lady Nottingham got up.

"Yes, I will go," she said. "Oh, Jeannie, you are not exaggerating things in your mind? Can't you tell me now?"

"No, my dear, it would take too long. Ah, there is Daisy."

A gentle tap sounded at the door; it was softly opened, and Daisy, seeing the light inside, came in.

"Ah, but how wicked of you, Aunt Jeannie," she said, "when you told me you were going to bed early. Yes, we are early too, but it was stupid and crowded, and so Gladys and I came away. Oh, you darling, it is nice to know you are here! But how tired you look!"

"Yes, dear, I am tired," said Jeannie. "I was just sending Aunt Alice away. And you must go away too. But it was dear of you just to look in to say good-night."

When the two had gone Jeannie sat down again in the window, her head resting on her hands, thinking vividly, intently.

"Thank Heaven she does not love him!" she said at length.

CHAPTER VIII.

The geography of breakfast at Lady Nottingham's was vague and shifting. Sometimes it all happened in the dining-room, sometimes, and rather oftener, little of it happened there, but took place, instead of on that continent, in the scattered islands of bedrooms. Gladys, however, was generally faithful to the continent, and often, as happened next morning, breakfasted there alone, while trays were carried swiftly upstairs to the bedrooms of the others. She alone of the inmates of the house had slept well that night. But she always slept well, even if she had the toothache.

Daisy had not slept at all well. It would be nearer the mark, indeed, to say that she had not even lain awake at all well, but had tossed and tumbled in a manner unprecedented. There was no wonder that it was unprecedented, since that which caused it had not occurred before to her. She had left the dance quite early, dragging Gladys away, because she had got something to think about which absorbed her. She had never been really absorbed before, though it was a chronic condition with her to be intensely and violently interested in a superficial manner. But this went deeper; from the springs of her nature now there came forth something both bitter and sweet, and tinged all her thoughts and her consciousness.

In herself, as she lay awake that night hearing the gradual diminuendo of the noises of traffic outside, till, when she thought there would be a hush, the crescendo of the work of the coming day began, she felt no doubt as to what this was which absorbed her and kept sleep so far aloof from her eyelids. It had started from as small a beginning as a fire that devastates a city, reducing it to desolation and blackened ash. A careless passenger has but thrown away the stump of a cigarette or a match not entirely extinguished near some inflammable material, and it is from no other cause than that that before long the walls of the tallest buildings totter and sway and fall, and the night is turned to a hell of burning flame. Not yet to her had come the wholesale burning, there was not yet involved in it all her nature; but something had caught fire at those few words of Lord Lindfield's; the heat and fever had begun.

Well she knew what it was that ailed her. Hitherto love was a thing that was a stranger to her, though she was no stranger to intense and impulsive affection like that which she felt for Aunt Jeannie. But how mysterious and unaccountable this was. It seemed to her that the phenomenon known as "love at first sight," of which she had read, was a thing far less to be wondered at. There a girl meets some one she has not seen before whom she finds holds for her that potent spell. That could be easily understood; the new force with which she comes in contact instantly exercises its power on her. But she, Daisy, had come across this man a hundred times, and now suddenly, without apparent cause, she who thought she knew him so well, and could appraise and weigh him and settle in her own mind, as she had done after her talk to Lady Nottingham the afternoon before, whether she would speak a word that for the rest of her life or his would make her fate and destiny, and fashion the manner of her nights and days, found that in a moment some change of vital import had come in turn on her, so that she looked on him with eyes of other vision, and thought of him in ways as yet undreamt of.

This was disquieting, unsettling; it was as if the house in which she dwelt—her own mind and body— which she had thought so well-founded and securely built—was suddenly shaken as by an earthquake shock, and she realized with a touch of panic-fear that outside her, and yet knit into her very soul, were forces unmanifested as yet which might prove to be of dominant potency.

Then, suddenly, her mood changed; their power was frightening no longer, they were wholly benignant and life-giving. It was not an earthquake shock that had frightened her, it was but the first beam of some new-rising sun that had struck on to the darkness of the world in which she had lived till now. She was smitten "by the first beam from the springing East," she who had never known before what morning was, or how fair was the light which it pours on to the world. And this morning beam was for her; it had not struck her fortuitously, shedding its light on her and others without choice. It had come to shine into her window, choosing that above all others. It was she that the first beam sought. It came to gild and glorify her house, her body and mind, the place where her soul dwelt.

How blind she had been! There was no difference in him; the difference had been in her alone. She had sat with sealed eyes at her window, or, at the most, with eyes that could but see the shadows and not the sun. Now they saw the sun only; there were no shadows, for the shadows had been but her own blindness.

Dawn was in the sky outside; here in the quiet, white-curtained room another dawn had come, not quiet, but with gleam of sun alternating with cloud and tempest, making the beholder wonder what the day would bring forth.

Aunt Jeannie, too, had lain long awake, but when sleep came it came deeply and dreamlessly, demanding the repair of two nights in the train and the agitation of her talk. She had given orders that she was not to be called till she rang, and when she woke the sun was already high, and the square outside lively with passengers and traffic. But it was with a sense of coming trial and trouble, if not quite of disaster, that she woke.

It was disaster she had to avert; she had to think and scheme. But had she known of Daisy's sleepless night, and the cause of that, she would have felt that the anchor which prevented the situation drifting into disaster had been torn up. For the anchor was the belief, as Lady Nottingham had told her, that Daisy was not in love with Tom Lindfield, and by one of fate's little ironies, at the very moment when she was comforting herself last night with that thought it was true no longer.

Her sleep had quite restored her, giving vigour to her body and the power of cool reflection to her brain, and when Victor came, according to promise, to see her during the morning there was no hint of trouble in her welcome of him, nor did he guess that any disquieting news had reached her. And his conclusion, though not actually true, was justly drawn, for the peace and the sense of security which she felt in his presence was of a kind that nothing else, except danger and disaster to it itself, could disturb.

It was a very tender, a very real part of her nature that was troubled, but the trouble did not reach down into these depths. Nor did she mean to speak of this trouble to him at all; a promise had been made by her to keep it as secret as could be. Hitherto the secret had been completely kept; it had passed the lips of none of the few who knew. But to-day she would be obliged to speak of it to Alice, for her plan to avert disaster was already half formed, but she dared not embark on it alone without counsel from another. For an utterly unlooked-for stroke of fate, supreme in its irony, that Daisy should be meditating marriage with the one man in the world whom it was utterly impossible that she should marry, had fallen, and at all costs the event must be averted.

CHAPTER IX.

The two girls, as had been already arranged, set off during the morning for the river-side house at Bray, where they would be joined next day by Lady Nottingham and the rest of her party; and Aunt Jeannie, returning home shortly before lunch, found that Daisy and Gladys had already gone, and that the hour for her consultation with her friend was come. For the situation admitted of no delay: in a sky that till yesterday had been of dazzling clearness and incomparable serenity there had suddenly formed this thunder-cloud, so to speak, hard, imminent, menacing. It was necessary, and immediately necessary (such was the image under which the situation presented itself to her mind), to put up a lightning-conductor over Daisy's room. It was the nature of the thunder-cloud that she had now to make known to Lady Nottingham: that done, between them they had to devise the lightning-conductor, or approve and erect that one which she had already designed in her mind during the sleepless hours of the night before. It was of strange design: she hardly knew if she had the skill to forge it. For the forging had to be done by her.

They lunched together, and immediately afterwards went to Lady Nottingham's sitting-room, where they would be undisturbed, for she had given orders that neither the most urgent of telephones nor the most intimate of callers were to be admitted. They drank their coffee in silence, and then Jeannie got up.

"I have got to tell you, Alice," she said, "about that which only yesterday I said I hoped I should never be obliged to speak of to anybody. I suppose the envious Fates heard me; certainly the words were scarcely out of my mouth before the necessity arose. What I have got to tell you about is that which all last autumn was harder for me to get over, I think, than all that I had been through myself. Only yesterday I believed it to be all dead; I believed it to be at most a memory from which time had already taken the bitterness. But I was completely and signally wrong. It is dead no longer; it is terribly alive, for it has had a resurrection which would convert a Sadducee. It is connected with the reason why Daisy can never marry Tom Lindfield. It is more than connected with it; it is the reason itself."

Jeannie had begun to speak standing by the fireplace and facing the full light of the window, but here she moved, and wheeling a chair with its back to the light, sat down in it. She wanted to be a voice and no more—a mere chronicle of a few hard, dry, irrevocable facts, things that had happened, and could not be altered or softened. There was no comment, no interpretation to be made. She had just to utter them; Alice Nottingham had just to hear them.

"You may have to give me time, my dear," she said, "for it will be as much as I can do, I am afraid, just to get through with the telling of it. Yes, I am already frightening you, I know. I do that on purpose, because I want to prepare you for a story that must shock and disturb you very much. I wondered last night whether I could manage without telling you, whether I could spare your hearing it all, but I find I can't. I can't act alone in this, on my own responsibility. Perhaps you may be able to think of some plan which will make mine unnecessary, and I would give a great deal for that to happen. But some plan must be made and carried out. Something has to be done."

She covered her face with her hands for a moment, then took them away, and spoke, slowly and carefully, so that there might be no need for further explanation of what she said.

"Of course you remember Diana, Daisy's sister," she said, "though you would remember her more as a name than as a person, for I think you never knew her at all well. She married very early, you know; she married that nice Frenchman, Monsieur Dupré. After that she lived abroad till the time of her death. The fact of that you will certainly remember, though it is now some years since it happened. Where are we? Yes, 1908. Then Diana died in 1903, five years ago. So at least we were told at the time. It was in 1903 that we, all of us, you, Daisy, and I, believed that Diana died."

Jeannie gave a long sigh.

"My story of why Daisy cannot marry Tom Lindfield has begun, dear Alice," she said, "for Diana did not die then. She lived for four years after that, and died last autumn only, in my arms, thank God! I thank God, my dear, that she died, and I thank God that I was with her. There was no one else, not her husband even."

Alice Nottingham turned on her a face that was puzzled, and was beginning to get frightened.

"But what does it all mean?" she said. "It is very disquieting, very strange, but what does it lead to? Daisy—Tom Lindfield."

"I am telling you as shortly as I can," said Jeannie. "Do not interrupt me, dear. It was last autumn she died, not five years ago as we had supposed. Five years ago she was—was found out, if you understand—she was found to have been living with another man not her husband.

He learned that, and he forgave her, for he adored her with a tender, unwavering devotion that is very rare. She was to him like a child who has been naughty and must be forgiven. Then in a few weeks only after that she fell again. Even then he did not divorce her, or make her bear the shame and publicity of what she had done; he simply let her go."

Jeannie was still speaking slowly and quietly, as if reading out some report which had to be mastered by her friend. But on the words "let her go" her voice trembled a little. But then she again recaptured the completeness of her self-control.

"Whether that was wise or not," she said, "whether it might not have been better if he had let Diana bear the punishment that human law has ordained for those poor things who behave as she behaved, we need not inquire. Nor need I tell you the details of how it was all managed, which I learned from Diana so few weeks before she died last year. It is sufficient for me to say that they left their home near Amiens together, ostensibly for a long foreign travel. After some weeks he sent home the news of her sudden death; he sent the news also to us in England. You were told, I and Daisy were told. And Diana, poor, poor Diana, went and lived in Paris."

Again the bravely-suppressed emotion made Jeannie's voice to quiver.

"That is what I mean when I said that M. Dupré let her go," she said. "Often I think it was a barbarous kindness. He could not live with her any more—the fact that he loved her so much made that impossible—and he had either to divorce her or—or let her vanish into the glittering crowd of those who—who are made like that. He chose the latter: he accounted for her disappearance by the news, sent to Amiens and sent to us in England, that she had died.

"So five years ago Diana went to Paris, and for a time lived, not with the man who had taken her from her husband, but with another. During her married life she had lived in that beautiful country-house of his near Amiens, seldom going to Paris, and no one apparently ever found out who she really was. Then——"

Again Jeannie paused—paused a long time; and before she spoke she put her hands over her eyes, as if to shut out some dreadful vision.

"Then she left that man," she said, "and lived with another. You know him; I know him; Daisy also."

It was as if Lady Nottingham had caught sight of that which made Jeannie cover her eyes, for she winced and drew back.

"Don't—don't!" she said; "I can't bear that, please, Jeannie!"

At the sound of the beseeching voice Jeannie recovered all her self-control. She was wanted; Alice wanted her for comfort.

"Oh, my dear, you must not be afraid," she said. "We have to face the facts and not be afraid of them, but do our best, and see how we can arrest or alter the train of their consequences. It was he—Tom Lindfield."

Again she paused, and again continued, speaking quietly.

"I knew nothing of all this till a little over a year ago," she said; "for even as M. Dupré had wished to spare Diana shame and publicity, so, I suppose, he wished to spare us the knowledge of what Diana had done, and it was thus that neither you nor Daisy nor I knew anything of it. I think perhaps he ought to have told us—told you and me, anyhow. But he did not, and it is of no use to think what we should have done if he had. But rather more than a year ago Diana herself wrote to me—wrote me a pitiful, heart-breaking letter. I thought at first it must be some grim practical joke, though I could not imagine who had played so cruel a trick, or why the trick had been played at all. But it was Diana's handwriting, and she enclosed a photograph of herself, which I have now. It was impossible to mistake that: nothing could mar her beauty; and then it was signed and dated in her own hand. She wrote to say that she had been ill, that she was getting rapidly worse—it was of consumption, perhaps you remember, that her mother died—and she wanted to know if I would come to her. She wanted to tell me everything, and, thank God, she wanted me. So it was there that I went when I left England last year.

"I stayed with her till she died in that little gilded flat. And during that month she told me everything. It—it was a long story, Alice, and it was all set to one shameful tune. And I was not shocked; that would have made my being with her quite useless, to begin with, but, also, I did not feel inclined to be shocked. She was so like a child—a child that has gone wrong, if you will, but still a child. Whether she was ashamed or not I hardly know, for after she had told me of it all we never once spoke of it again. Certainly she wished, as passionately as she was capable in her poor dying state of wishing anything, that she should not bring shame or sorrow on others. Of all others that she wished to spare, most of all she wished to spare Daisy; and—a promise to a dying person is a very solemn thing—I promised that I would do all that lay in my power so that Daisy should not know. Till yesterday I thought that promise would never come up. But it has. Daisy must not conceivably marry him. Also, she must not know why. There is our crux.

"And one word more, in justice to him," she added. "I am convinced he does not to this day know who it was with whom he lived in Paris. He knew me, for instance, and liked me; and I am sure he would not have lived with her knowing who she was. Oh, but, Alice, the misery, the sorrow of it all! You don't know. You weren't with Diana at the end. And I loved her. And I think her—her going so utterly wrong like that made me love her more. The pity of it! The hopeless, helpless sorrow of it! She did not want to die——"

Jeannie's voice choked for a moment.

"She wanted life, she wanted love, poor child. She was like some beautiful wild thing, without law. She didn't think. She never loved her husband, who adored her. She didn't think. And she died frightened—frightened at what might be in front of her. As if the

Infinite Tenderness was not in front of her! As if Jesus Christ, the Man of many sorrows, was not there! Oh, Alice, how can we judge?"

"Ah, my dear, we don't judge," said she. "Anyhow, no judgment of ours has any effect. It is done with as far as she is concerned."

Jeannie's face suddenly brightened into a semblance of a smile. It was veiled, but it was but the flesh that veiled it; at the core it was wholly loving.

"Then we are content to leave dear Diana in the hands of the Infinite Pity?" she said. "That must be certain before we can talk further."

"But with my whole heart," said Lady Nottingham.

Again there was silence; and in that Jeannie openly dried the tears that were on her face. She had been crying: there was no question about that.

"I had to tell you, dear Alice," she said at length. "I could not bear it alone. You see why it is impossible, beyond the bounds of speech, that Daisy should marry him. You see also why I thank Heaven that she does not love him. At all costs, also, Daisy must not know why it is impossible. That was my promise to Diana when she was dying. I would do anything within my power and the stretched-out limits of it to prevent her knowing. Diana, poor darling, wished for that. It was the last request she made. It is sacred to me, as sacred as my honour."

"Do you mean to tell him?" asked Alice.

"I hope not to. I want to keep poor Diana's secret as close as can be. And I am not in the least certain, from what I know of him, that it would do any good. If he wants Daisy, do you think a man like that would let that stand in his way? No, we must do better than that. Now, is he in love with her?"

"I can't say. It is clear, however, that he wants to marry her. He has been in love so many times that one doubts if he has been in love at all. There was——"

"Oh, spare me the list of his conquests. He has been in love many times. That is sufficient."

"Sufficient for what?"

"For the plan that has occurred to me as possible. I don't say it is easy; I don't say it is nice; but we want, above all things, to keep poor Diana's dreadful secret, to let no one, if possible—and, above all, Daisy—know that it was her sister who lived those years in Paris, and in that manner."

Jeannie got up.

"Clearly the easiest way of arriving at what we want is to make Daisy think that he has only been flirting with her," she said—"that he is not serious. It will hurt the poor child, I know; but if she were in love with him, which you think she is not, it would hurt her far, far more. Therefore, we must waste no time. Any day, any moment, she may fall in love with him. He is extremely attractive."

"Do you mean you will tell Daisy that he has only been flirting with her?" asked Alice.

"No, that would do no good. She would not believe it. Besides, any day also he may propose to her. No, it must be more convincing than that. She must see that which convinces her that he is not in earnest. We must make him, if we can, under Daisy's very nose, flirt with somebody else. We must make him neglect her. I don't know if it can be done, but we must try. At least, I can think of no other plan which will not involve telling Daisy all that we want to keep from her."

"But how—who?" asked Alice.

"He is coming to Bray—Lord Lindfield, I mean?"

"Yes; he is coming to-morrow evening with the others."

Jeannie paused in front of a mirror, looked long at herself, and spoke to her image there.

"Yes, passable yet—just passable yet," she said to herself.

Lady Nottingham got up and came across the room to her.

"Jeannie, what do you mean?" she asked. "What is it you mean?"

Jeannie turned round quickly.

"Ah! you guess," she said. "I don't say it is nice; I shan't like myself much, I can promise you. But it is not so long since he ran after me a good deal. Perhaps you remember the fact. He didn't receive much encouragement then. Well, I mean that he shall do it again. This time he shall receive much more encouragement. I will make it very easy for him. I will help him a great deal now. I will flirt with him all the time at Bray. Flirt—yes. Oh, it is not a nice word, and flirts are not nice people, as we settled only yesterday. We settled they were not worth talking about. But I am going to be one now—and a bad one, too—under Daisy's very nose. Perhaps I shan't succeed, but I shall do my best; and if I don't succeed, we must try to think of something else. But I want Daisy to see how easily and readily he makes love to a woman. I want her to see herself slighted and neglected. I want her to be hurt— and finally to be angry, to be furious, to see that he means nothing. Then, provided only she is not in love with him now, she will hate and despise him."

Jeannie spoke rapidly, excitedly, her face flushing.

"Or do you think it is a forlorn hope, Alice?" she said. "Am I but flattering myself that I am not quite *passée* yet? Oh, it is a heavy handicap, I know, for a woman of my age to try to cut out a brilliant young girl, and one who is beautiful; and, as you have told me, he never, as far as you know, flirted with a girl. Well, that proves he likes women best."

"Ah! but you can't do it, Jeannie," broke in Lady Nottingham. "Think of what you will appear to Daisy; think of your own self-respect; think of Victor. What will he make of it all? It is too dangerous."

"I have thought of all those things," said Jeannie. "I have weighed and balanced them; and they seem to me lighter than that promise I made to Diana. I may have to tell Victor; about that I don't know, but I shall do my utmost not to. It may not be necessary, for, Alice, I think he trusts me as utterly as I trust him. I think that if I saw him running after some other woman I should feel there must be some explanation, and I hope I should not ask him for it, or think he was faithless to me. And I believe he has that trust in me also. I don't know. If he demands to know what it all means I shall tell him, because if you are asked anything in the name of love it is not possible to refuse. Heaven knows, this is a desperate measure! But show me any other that has a chance of success and will still keep Diana's secret. This may fail; one cannot be sure of any plan going right. But show me any other plan at all, and from the bottom of my heart I will thank you."

Lady Nottingham shook her head.

"I can think of no other plan," she said; "but I can't approve of this one. You are playing with serious things, Jeannie; you are playing with love and other people's souls. Diana did not mean you to do anything like this in order to keep your promise to her."

"No, poor child! One does not easily see the consequences of one's acts, or how they go on long after they are committed, bringing joy or sorrow to others. Oh, Alice, there is such a dreadful vitality about evil. Acts that one thinks are all over and dead have an awful power of coming to life again. What one has done never dies. It may be forgiven—Heaven grant it may be forgiven—but it exists still in the lives of others."

"But it is not as if she were alive," said the other, "or as if she could suffer for it."

Jeannie shook her head.

"Ah, my dear," she said, "to my mind that is a reason the more for keeping my promise. Living people can defend themselves to some extent, or you can appeal to them and make them see, perhaps, that such a promise involves more than it is reasonable to demand. But the dead, Alice! The dead are so defenceless!"

Lady Nottingham was silent, knowing that it is useless to argue over questions of feeling; for no amount of reasoning, however admirable, can affect a question about which the heart has taken sides. And after a moment Jeannie went on:—

"And it is not the dead alone," she said. "There is Daisy also to consider. Had I made no promise at all, I think I would do anything as distasteful and odious to me as that which I am going to do, for the sake of keeping that dreadful knowledge from her. Alice, think if you had had a sister like that! Could you ever get rid of the poison of it? And it is an awful thing to let a young soul be poisoned. When we grow older, we get, I suppose, better digestions; poisons affect us less. That is the worst of growing old."

Again she paused.

"And now, dear—as they say at the end of sermons—let us talk no more about it. You will see me in an odious rôle down at Bray; but it will be something to know that you are aware it is a rôle, an odious rôle assumed for a good purpose. I shall seem detestable to Daisy, and she will not be able to believe her eyes, until she is forced to. I shall seem charming to him, Tom Lindfield, until at the end, when, as we hope, Daisy is convinced, I shall turn round like the flirt and say, 'What do you mean?' I shall seem odious to myself, but I do not believe I shall seem odious to Victor. I think he will know there is something he does not understand. Perhaps I shall do it all very badly, and not succeed in detaching him at all from Daisy. It is true I have not had much practice, for I assure you I am not a flirt by nature. Oh, Alice, can't you think of any other plan? I can't, and I have thought so hard. Have you got a very large party? I don't want a full house to witness this disgusting performance. I shall have to be so cheap. I wish Victor was not going to be there. At least, I am not sure. I think he will see he does not understand. It is bad luck, you know, that of all men in the world this should be the one whom Daisy thinks about marrying. Now let us dismiss it altogether."

Lady Nottingham felt a certain sense of injustice.

"Dear Jeannie," she said, "you have done all the talking, and, having expressed your views, you say, 'Let us dismiss it altogether.' By all means, if you choose; but I haven't had a chance. You have prophesied success to your scheme; I prophesy disaster. You are not fitted for your rôle; you will break down long before you accomplish anything. You will see Daisy looking at you with reproach; you will see Victor looking at you with wonder; you will see Lord Lindfield looking at you with—with admiration. You won't be able to bear any of those things, least of all the last. You will have some involuntary shudder of horror at him, or you will obey your heart and run to comfort Daisy, and give it all away.

Yours is one of the schemes that don't come off, because they are unthinkable."

But Jeannie interrupted again.

"You mustn't discourage me," she said, "because I want all the spirits I am capable of to carry it through. It has to be done with a light heart, else it will deceive nobody. And so, my dear, to-morrow you will say 'good-bye' to me, and have a sort of wraith of me instead for a little while. Oh, Alice, I hope it won't take very long!"

The intense heat of the afternoon had a little abated, and after tea the two drove out for a while, returning early in order to dine and go to the opera. It began at eight, and Jeannie, after her year's sojourn in the country, demanded a full dose, and they arrived before the beginning of the first act. Outside it was still not quite the hour of sunset, and the streets and houses were gilded by the soft reddish glow of the superb summer evening. At the porch of the opera-house were a few men standing about, clearly waiting for friends, and for that purpose examining the disembarking carriages. As the two got out, one of these gently but quite firmly shouldered his way towards them.

"Looking out for an acquaintance, I find a friend, Lady Nottingham," he said. "That's my luck all over.—

Why, Mrs. Halton! Have you the smallest remembrance of me?"

Jeannie had seen him, and for one moment of weakness and indecision had tried to pass by without seeming to recognize him. But it was impossible to ignore this, and though she had hoped her rôle would not begin till to-morrow, it was clear now that she must start to-day.

"Why, but how charming to see you, Lord Lindfield," she said. "I am delighted. I am only just home, you know—or perhaps you don't, for why should you? Do leave your acquaintance in the lurch, now you have found a friend—it would have been prettier of you, by the way, to have said two friends—and join us. Alice dear, carry Lord Lindfield off under your cloak to the box. Kidnap him."

"Jove! yes, I'll be kidnapped," said he. "Kidnap me quick, please, Lady Nottingham, because I see Mrs. Streatham's carriage. Too late; she sees me. May I come up for—for an hour or two, after the first act?"

"Not for an hour, for two," said Jeannie, as Mrs. Streatham waved her hand to him, but without a smile, for she was busy wondering who Mrs. Halton was, and whether there was a chance of getting her to dine two or three times during the next week.

Mrs. Streatham used her friends and acquaintances much as a clematis uses the wires or trellis put up for it. She strongly and firmly climbed along them (without ever letting go), to find fresh friends and acquaintances.

"Who was that charming-looking woman you were talking to, Lord Lindfield," she said, "with Lady Nottingham? By the way, you lunch with us on Thursday, do you not?"

"Mrs. Halton," said he.

"Really! That sweetly pretty Miss—Miss Hanbury's aunt? Are she and Lady Nottingham in the stalls? They might like to come to my box instead. It is so far more comfortable in a box. Will you ask them? I do know Lady Nottingham. She dined with us last year—at least, I asked her."

"They have a box of their own," said he.

"Ah, what a pity! Let us go in. I expect a few friends this evening, but they will find their way. It is such a pity to miss a note of 'Faust.' Oh, I see, it is 'Lucia.' That is by Gounod too, is it not?"

Three hours later they were all standing in the vestibule waiting for the arrival of carriages. Mrs. Streatham had been unable to arrange anything definite with regard to Mrs. Halton lunching with her, but had just said she would write, and hope to find her disengaged the week after next, when her carriage was bawled out. Lord Lindfield shut her firmly into it, with profuse thanks, and returned to the others. Crowds of people—some of whom, apparently, Mrs. Streatham did not know by sight—had swarmed into her box during the evening, and he had spent most of it in Lady Nottingham's without any sense of deserting his hostess, since it was impossible even to stand in her box, far less sit down.

Then Lady Nottingham's carriage had come up too, and he put them into it.

"Till to-morrow, then," said Jeannie. "I am looking forward to it immensely. You lunch with us first, and then take me to the concert."

The motor bubbled and slid off, and she put down the window.

"It moves," she said laconically.

CHAPTER X.

Lady Nottingham's house at Bray was one of those styleless nondescript river-side residences which, apart from the incomparable beauty of their surroundings, have a charm of their own, elusive but distinct. Originally it had been no more than a couple of cottages, thatched and low-eaved, but her husband in his lifetime had dealt with these so successfully by building out a dining-room with bedrooms above on one side, a drawing-room and billiard-room, again with bedrooms above, on the other, and a long row of servants' rooms and offices, that now it was commodious enough to take in a tolerably large party in extreme comfort.

It is true that he might have built something quite as commodious at far less expense by pulling down the old and beginning again, but, on the other hand, the amusement and employment he got out of it was cheap at the additional price.

The house stood screened from the river by a thick-set hawthorn hedge, inside which was a garden of a couple of acres in extent, in which was combined the charm of antiquity with the technique of skilful modern gardening. Unlike many English gardens, which are laid out to be active in, this was clearly a place for the lazy and the lounger. There were no tennis courts, no croquet lawns, no place, in fact, where any game could be played that demanded either extent or uniformity of surface. A wavy, irregular lawn, all bays and angles and gulfs of green, was fitted into the headlands and promontories of garden beds, as the sea is fitted into the land; but the voyager never got to open sea, so to speak, but was always turning round corners into other gulfs.

It was impossible to imagine a place less formally laid out, or one, considering the extent of it, where you could walk so short a way in the same direction.

There were no straight lines anywhere, an omission fatal in the eyes of a formalist, but paths, broad paths of grass, or narrower paths of old paving-stone, meandered about in a manner that could hardly fail to please.

On each side of such paths were garden beds, no mere ribbons, but wide, deep spaces of well-nourished earth, where just now June made jungle. Here you could sit and become part of the general heat and fragrance, and lose your identity in summer, or, moving a little, find a tree, no shrub, but a big living elm in tower of leaf and panoply of spreading bough, to be cool under. Pigeons from the big dovecot in front of the house afforded to a leisure mind a sufficiency of general conversation, or formed a cooing chorus of approval if anybody wished to talk himself; but one thing clearly prohibited in these warm, green places was to be active. The actively inclined had to pass through the gate in the hedge, and there, by turning to the left, they would find a back-water with a whole village of boat-houses. There, to suit the measure of their activity, they could equip themselves with the required materials; there were punts at their disposal, or they could take unto themselves a canoe, or a portly, broad-beamed ark, or risk themselves in outriggers of extreme length and uncertain stability.

The house itself afforded no less scope for the various inclinations of its inhabitants. There was a charming drawing-room where any one could sit up, take notice, and be formal. There was an immense billiard-room, with an alcove containing a couple of card tables, so far away from the billiards that the sound of cannons reached the ear of the bridge-player in a manner that could not disconcert; while for wet days and the more exuberantly inclined there was a squash-racquet court where any amount of exercise could be enjoyed with the smallest possible expenditure of time.

The two original cottages had been run together, and a hall now comprised the whole ground floor of both. Wooden joists of the floors above made parallels down the ceiling, and it was still lit through the small-paned windows of the original cottages, through the squares of which the landscape outside climbed up and down over the ridges of the glass. At one end was the fireplace, which had once been a kitchen-range; but that removed, a large open hearth, burning a wood fire when fires were necessary, was flanked by two settles within the chimney-space.

At the other end, and facing it, the corresponding kitchen range of the second cottage had also been cleared out, but the chimney above it had been boarded in, and a broad, low settee ran round the three sides of it. Above this settee, and planted into the wall, so that the heads of those uprising should not come in contact with the shelves, was a bookcase full of delectable volumes, all fit to be taken down at random, and opened at random, all books that were familiar friends to any who had friends among that entrancing family. Tennyson was there, and all Thackeray; Omar Khayyam was there, and Alice in Wonderland; Don Quixote rubbed covers with John Inglesant, and Dickens found a neighbour in Stevenson.

But this was emphatically a room to sit down in, not to move about in, for the levels of the floor were precarious, and a sudden step would easily disconcert those who tried to make a promenade of it. It was as inactive in tendency as the garden.

Outside the house was charmingly irregular. The billiard-room with the bedrooms above it was so markedly Queen Anne that it was impossible to believe it could be Queen Anne. Nor was it, for it was Queen Victoria. Then came the cottage section, which had a thatched roof, on which grew wallflowers and the pink pincushions of valerian, and following that was a low, stern line of building containing kitchens and servants' rooms, which made no pretence to be anything except that which it was.

But over pseudo-Queen Anne, genuine George I. cottages, and frankly Edwardian kitchens, there rose a riot of delectable vegetation. White jasmine and yellow jasmine strove together like first cousins who hate each other, jackmanni and tropæolum were rival beauties, and rambler roses climbed indifferently about, made friends where they could, and when they found themselves unable, firmly stabbed their enemies and strangled their remains.

Charming, however, as it all was, it had no mood to suggest. It but accentuated the moods of those who came there, and by its very vagueness and softness reflected the spirits of its visitors. It was impossible to imagine a place more conducive to foster and cherish a man's inclinations; to the lover it would be a place ideal for a honeymoon, to the studious an admirable study. In the Italian phrase the whole place was *simpatico*; it repeated and crooned over to every one the mood in which he came to it. And if a lover would find it an adorable setting for his beloved and himself, so, too, it would mock and rail in sympathy with one who was cynical and bitter. But since most people are not in any particular mood, and when they come into the country require light and agreeable diversion, Lord Nottingham had been quite right in providing so ample a billiard-room, so engaging a library, so varied a fleet of river-craft.

Daisy and Gladys had come down here the day before Lady Nottingham and the rest of the party were to arrive, and they found plenty to occupy them. The house had not been used since Easter, and wore that indescribable look of uninhabitableness which results from a thorough house-cleaning. Everything, even in the irregular hall, looked angular and uncomfortable; chairs were set square to tables; tables were set at mathematically precise angles; blinds were all drawn down exactly four inches from the tops of the windows; and all the books were in their shelves.

It was all too tidy to have been lived in, and, therefore, too tidy to live in, and it took Daisy nearly an hour to take the chill off the room, as she put it, though the heat here was nearly as intense as it had been in town. Gladys, who was no good at this subtle business of restoring life to a dead room, occupied herself with writing out the names of the guests very neatly on cards, which she then, with equal neatness, affixed to the doors of their rooms.

Daisy paused at the end of this hour and surveyed the room with satisfaction. "For one who has till so lately been a corpse it isn't bad," she said. "Don't you see the difference, Gladys? It was like a refrigerator before. Yes, let's have tea at once, shall we, and then go out? There's lots more to do. We must pick great boughs of laburnum and beech for all the big vases. Gardeners are no good at that; nor are you, dear, for that matter. You tell them to pick boughs, and they pick button-holes."

"I hate picking flowers at all," said Gladys. "They are so much nicer where they are."

Daisy poured out tea.

"I know you think that," she said, "and I entirely disagree. Whenever you see flowers in a house you think what a pity they are not growing in the garden; whereas, whenever I see flowers in a garden, it seems to me such a pity they are not in the house. Of course, when the house is quite, quite full, I don't mind the rest remaining in the garden."

Gladys laughed.

"I think that's like you," she said. "You want to use things on the whole, and I on the whole want to let them enjoy themselves."

"That sounds as if you thought yourself a perfect saint of unselfishness and me a greedy pig," remarked Daisy. "If you don't come to tea I shall eat all the strawberries. Perhaps you wish they had never been picked, and left to rot on their stems by way of enjoying themselves."

Gladys finished the last name on her packet of cards for guests' rooms.

"No, I don't go as far as that," she said, "because I like the taste of them, which you can't get at unless you eat them. Now flowers look much nicer when they are growing."

"Yes, but they are not yours so much when they are growing," said Daisy. "I like them in my house, in my vases. Yes, I suppose I am greedy. Oh, I am going to enjoy myself these next few days. All the people I like best are coming, and they mostly like me best. That is such an advantage. Wouldn't it be awful to like somebody very much and find he didn't like you? What a degrading position! Oh dear, what a nice world!"

"More than usual?"

"Much more. I'm dreadfully happy inside. Don't you know how you can be immensely happy outside and not really be happy at all? But when you are happy inside you are happy altogether, and don't mind a wet day or going to the dentist's one scrap. Isn't it funny how one gets happy inside all in a moment? I suppose there is a cause for everything, isn't there? Ugh! there's an earwig. Oh, it's going your way, not mine. I wonder what the cause of earwigs is. I wish they would find it out and reason it away."

Gladys put an empty inverted teacup over the earwig.

"What made you happy inside?" she asked.

"Well, darling Aunt Alice started it two afternoons ago when we came back from the Zoo. I had a delightful talk, and she gave me some excellent advice. She quite realized that I wasn't exactly what most people would call being in love with him, but she advised me anyhow to make up my mind whether I would say 'yes' or 'no,' and recommended 'yes.' And so I did make up my mind, and the very next day, do you know, Gladys, when I dragged you away from the ball so early———"

"Because you had a headache," said Gladys, ruthlessly.

She had been enjoying herself, and still a little resented Daisy's imperious order to go away.

"You needn't rub it in, darling. Well, that very night something happened to me that frightened me at first. I began to feel quite differently about him."

Daisy got up quickly.

"I've been so dreadfully happy ever since," she said, "although sometimes I've felt quite miserable. Do you see the difference, or does it sound nonsense? Let me explain. I've only felt miserable, but I was happy. Gladys, I do believe it's It. It does make one feel so infinitesimal, and so immense."

Gladys looked up quickly at her cousin. Whatever It was, this was certainly a Daisy who was quite strange to her—Daisy with a strange, shy look in her eyes, half exulting in this new feeling, half ashamed of it.

"I hardly slept at all that night," she said, "and yet the night didn't seem in the least long. And I don't think I wanted to sleep except now and then when I felt miserable. And I believe it's the same thing that makes me feel miserable which makes me so happy. Gladys, I shall be so shy of him to-morrow when he comes here that he will probably think I'm in the sulks. And he's coming early probably, before any of the others—before lunch, in fact."

Gladys got up.

"Oh, Daisy, I don't think you ought to have arranged that," she said. "Do you mean he will find just you and me here?"

Daisy laughed.

"He needn't find you unless you like," she said. "And I didn't exactly arrange it. I told him you and I would be alone here, and he asked if he might get down early. I couldn't exactly forbid him; besides, darling, I didn't want to."

"Mother wouldn't like it," said Gladys.

"So please don't tell her," remarked Daisy. "I hate vexing people. She won't find out either. We shall go on the river or something, and come back after the rest of the people have arrived. You are so old-fashioned, Gladys; besides, it isn't certain that he will come. He only said he would if he could. But he is the sort of man who usually can when he wishes."

"I ought to tell mother," said Gladys.

"I know, but you won't."

Daisy laughed again, and then suddenly, without reason, her spirits fell.

"Oh dear, what a little beast I have been!" she said. "I did arrange that he should come, Gladys; at least, I made it imperative that he should ask if he might, and now it seems so calculating and cold-blooded. Girls like whom I used to be till—till about forty-eight hours ago are such brutes. They plot and scheme and entrap men. Pigs! I almost hope he won't come. I do, really. And yet that wouldn't do either, for it would look as if he had found me out and was disgusted with me. I believe you are all wrong, both you and Aunt Alice, and that he doesn't care for me in the least. He has flirted with half London. It isn't his fault; women have always encouraged him, just as I have done. What beasts we are!"

"Oh, well, come and pick boughs of laburnum," said Gladys. "Let's go and do something. We've been indoors all the afternoon."

"But I don't want to pick boughs of laburnum," said Daisy. "Why should we do the gardener's work? I want to cry."

"Very well, cry," said Gladys. "Oh, Daisy, I'm not a brute. I am so sorry you feel upset. But you know you are very happy; you have told me so. I should like to be immensely sympathetic, but you do change so quickly, I can't quite keep up. It must be very puzzling. Do you suppose everybody is like you when she falls in love?"

"And I wish I was dead," said Daisy, violently, having arrived at that dismal conclusion by some unspoken train of thought. "I wish I was a cow. I wish I was a boy."

"But you can't be a cow or a boy," said Gladys, gravely, "and you don't really wish you were dead."

Daisy suddenly had a fit of the giggles, which before long infected her cousin also, and they both lay back in their chairs in peals of helpless laughter. Now and then one or other would recover a little, only to be set off again by the temporarily hopeless case, and it was not till they had laughed themselves tired that the fit subsided.

Daisy mopped her streaming eyes.

"L-let's pick laburnum," she said at length. "How silly you are! But it would save such a lot of trouble to be a cow. If I laugh any more I shall be sick."

"Come into the garden, then," said Gladys. "Oh dear! I didn't mean *that*. Don't laugh again, Daisy; it does hurt so dreadfully."

CHAPTER XI.

Whatever might prove to be the conduct of others, it seemed clear next morning that the weather meant to do all in its power to help Daisy to have a happy time, and another hot and cloudless day succeeded. The girls intended originally to lunch at one, since that gave a longer afternoon; but at one, since nobody had appeared, it seemed wiser to put off lunch till half-past, since that was the hour at which they lunched in London. Eventually they sat down alone to a meal even more belated. But at present nothing could touch or mar Daisy's happiness.

"It is much better that he shouldn't come," she said, with an air of decision. "I daresay Aunt Alice wouldn't like it, though it couldn't have been supposed to be my fault. Very likely his motor has broken down; he told me it usually did."

She laughed quite naturally; there was no sting in his absence.

"In fact, he told me he usually sent it on ahead," she said, "and started walking after it about half an hour later. In that way, by the time he arrived his chauffeur had generally put it to rights again, and he got in."

"Then he ought to be here in half an hour," remarked Gladys.

"Yes. Shall we have lunch kept cold for him? It would be hot by the time he arrived if we didn't. Oh, Gladys, I believe you are laughing at me. How horrid of you!"

"Not in the least. But I am rather glad he didn't come. I hate concealing things from mother."

Daisy put her nose in the air.

"Oh, you needn't have worried. He would have been quite certain to have told Aunt Alice himself."

"You didn't think of that yesterday," said Gladys.

"No. What disgusting salad! I believe it's made of turnip-tops. I'm very glad he didn't come to lunch."

"Men are so greedy about their food," said Gladys. "I don't mind what I eat."

"Evidently, since you can eat that. Oh, Gladys, I don't mean to be cross, but when you say things on purpose to annoy me it would be such bad manners in me not to appear to be annoyed. Do you think his motor has broken down? Fancy him tramping down the Bath road on a day like this! He hates walking unless he is going to kill something. He was charged by a rhinoceros once. If you try to shoot them and miss, they charge. How awfully tiresome of them! He killed it afterwards, though. It was quite close. You never heard anything so exciting."

Gladys laughed.

"Oh, Daisy," she said, "you told me that before, and you said it was so hard to know what to say if you didn't know a rhinoceros from a hippopotamus. And now you find it too exciting."

"Well, what then?" said Daisy, with dignity. "I think one ought to take an interest in all sorts of subjects. It is frightfully suburban only to be interested in what happens in your own parish. Somebody said that the world was his parish."

"I don't know what parish Grosvenor Square is in," said Gladys, parenthetically.

Somehow Daisy, in this new mood, was far less formidable than the glittering crystal which had been Daisy up till now. She seemed to have rubbed shoulders with the world, instead of streaking the sky above it. Her happiness, you would say, even in the moment of its birth, had humbled and softened her. Gladys found she had not the slightest fear of being snapped up. Several times during lunch Daisy had snapped, but she had snapped innocuously. They had finished now, and she rose.

"I expect him in about an hour," said Daisy, rather magisterially. "Let us finish the flowers. I love flowers in my bedroom, don't you? Do let us put a dish of them in everybody's bedroom. It looks so welcoming. Books, too; everybody likes a book or two in his room. It's so easy to do little things like that, and people appreciate it enormously. There's the whole of the afternoon before us; nobody will arrive till the five o'clock train."

"But I thought you said you expected him——" began Gladys.

"Darling, pray don't criticize my last remark but three. Every remark becomes obsolete as soon as another remark is made."

Daisy's last conjecture was correct, and it was not till after five, when tea had been laid on the broad, creeper-covered verandah to the east of the house, that any one appeared. Then, however, they appeared in large numbers, for most of Lady Nottingham's guests had chosen the train she recommended to travel by. Every one, in fact, arrived by it with the exception of Jeannie Halton and Lord Lindfield.

"I knew Jeannie would miss it," Lady Nottingham said, "but as she was equally certain she would not the thing had to be put to the proof. Daisy darling, how are you? She insisted on being taken to the symphony concert; at least, she didn't so much insist as Lord Lindfield insisted on taking her. They were to meet us at Paddington, and in case—Jeannie went so far as to provide for that contingency—in case they missed it, he was to drive her down in his motor."

Victor Braithwaite, who had come with the party, joined in.

"I know that motor," he said. "It can do any journey the second time it tries, but no journey the first time. He took me the other day from Baker Street to South Audley Street, and it stuck in the middle of Oxford Street."

Jim Crowfoot helped himself largely to strawberries, and turned to Daisy. He was a slim, rather small young man, with a voice some two sizes too large for him. He was supposed to be rather a good person to have in the house, because he never stopped talking. Had it been possible to cover him over with a piece of green baize, like a canary, when one had had enough, he would have been even more desirable.

"I suppose that's what they mean by second thoughts being the best," he said. "It isn't usually the case; at least, I find that if ever I think right, it's always when I don't give the matter any consideration. I came down here without considering that I promised to dine with Mrs. Streatham this evening, and it was an excellent plan."

Mrs. Beaumont broke in. Her plan was always to be tremendously appreciative of everybody for two sentences, in order to enhance the effect of the nasty things she said of everybody the moment afterwards. It set the nasty things off better.

"I think every one is too horrid about our dear kind Mrs. Streatham," she said. "She is the most hospitable woman I know, and you, for instance, Jim, go and eat her cutlets and then laugh at her. She asked me to dine with her next Friday, but I said I couldn't, as I remembered I was already engaged. When I looked at my book I found it was with her that I had already promised to dine. I like being asked twice; it shows one is really wanted."

"Oh, we're all really wanted," said Jim. "But we don't always want the people who want us. That is the tragedy. If you'll ask me to dinner once, Mrs. Beaumont, I will transfer two of Mrs. Streatham's invitations to you."

"There you are again! You are not kind. It would upset her table."

"Not at all. Her husband would dine downstairs, and her daughter would dine upstairs. That is the advantage of having a family. You can always make things balance."

"I have a family," said she, "and that is exactly why my bank-book won't balance. But when I overdraw I always threaten to transfer my account. Bankers will stand anything but that, won't they, Mr. Braithwaite? Let us go and stroll. Dear Jim always talks so loud that I can't hear myself think. And if I don't hear myself think I don't know what I shall say next. Do tell me, was it on purpose, do you think, that Mrs. Halton and Lord Lindfield missed their train? I may be quite wrong, but didn't you think that Alice said it as if she had rather expected it?"

"Surely, she said she expected it."

"How interesting! What a heavenly garden! I only have just met Mrs. Halton. Every one says she is too fascinating."

"She is perfectly charming," said he. "Is that the same thing?"

"Oh, not at all; you may be perfectly charming without being the least fascinating. No man ever wants to marry a perfectly charming woman; they only think it delightful when one of their friends does so."

Daisy had heard most of this as the two left the verandah and strolled off down the garden, and the effect that it had on her was to make her label Mrs. Beaumont as "horrid." She was quite aware that three-quarters of the ordinary light conversation that went on between people who were not friends but only acquaintances was not meant to be taken literally, and that no one of any perception took it otherwise. Tribute to Aunt Jeannie's charms had been paid on both sides; the woman had heard of her as "too fascinating," Victor had found her charming. Daisy herself, from her own point of view, could find no epithet too laudatory, and she endorsed both the "fascinating" and the "charming." But she was just conscious that she would have preferred that Victor should have called her fascinating, and Mrs. Beaumont charming, rather than that it should have been the other way about.

But it was not because Mrs. Beaumont called her fascinating that Daisy labelled that unconscious lady as horrid; it was because she had made the suggestion that Lord Lindfield and her aunt had missed the train on purpose, in order, so it followed, that they should drive down together in the motor whose second thoughts were so admirable. Daisy scorned the insinuation altogether; she felt that she degraded herself by allowing herself to think of it. But that had been clearly implied.

The group round the tea-table had dispersed, and she easily found herself next Aunt Alice.

"Everything is in order, dear Aunt Alice," she said, "and Gladys has worked so hard. But I don't think I should have come down yesterday if I had known there was a symphony concert this afternoon. What did they have?"

"Brahms, I think," said Lady Nottingham, vaguely. "There is Brahms, isn't there? Neither Jeannie nor Lord Lindfield quite knew. They went to see."

"But when did they settle to go and see?" asked Daisy.

"Last night, I think. Oh, yes, at the Opera last night.—Yes, Mr. Crowfoot, of course you may have another cup. Sugar?—He came to my box—Lord Lindfield, I mean—and was so delighted to meet your Aunt Jeannie again.—Yes, I put in one lump, Mr. Crowfoot. Is that right?"

Lady Nottingham certainly succeeded admirably in the lightness of touch she gave to the little speech. She knew, as well as if Daisy had told her in so many words, the sort of feeling that had dictated Daisy's rather catechism-questions about the manner of Jeannie and Lindfield settling to go to the concert, and what there was at the concert. But the lightness of touch was not easy; she knew quite well, and did not fail to remember, that a few days ago only she had advised Daisy to have her answer ready when (not "if") Lord Lindfield proposed to her. He had certainly not done so, but Daisy had evidently not expected him to go to a concert with her aunt and miss his train and drive down with her. She had no reason to suppose that anything that could be called jealousy was as yet existent in Daisy's mind. She only, perhaps, wanted to know exactly what had happened.

Jim Crowfoot had only paused like a bird on the wing, pouncing on morsels of things to eat, and having got his second cup of tea he flew off again instantly to Mrs. Majendie, whom he was regaling with a shrill soliloquy. Thus for a moment Daisy and Aunt Alice were alone at the tea-table.

Daisy dropped into a chair at Lady Nottingham's side.

"I am so glad he likes Aunt Jeannie," she said in her best and quickest style, "and that she likes him. I suppose they do like each other, since they go to a concert together and miss a train together. You never miss trains with people you don't like, do you, Aunt Alice? I was rather afraid, do you know, that Aunt Jeannie wouldn't like him. I am so glad I was wrong. And they knew each other before, did they?"

Lady Nottingham paused a moment. She never devoted, as has been said, more of her brain than was necessary to deal with the subject in hand, but it appeared to her that a good deal of brain was required here. Daisy, poor undiplomatic Daisy, had tried so hard in this rapid, quick-witted little speech to say all the things she knew she ought to feel, and which, as a matter of fact, she did not feel. Superficially, it was no doubt delightful that Aunt Jeannie should like Tom Lindfield; it was delightful also that he should like her. The speech was all quite correct, quite sincere as far as it went, but if one took it further it was all quite insincere. She said all that the surface felt in order to conceal what she really felt.

And the light reply again was not easy to Lady Nottingham. She had considered Jeannie's plan in all its bearings, and neither then nor now could she think of a better plan. But already Daisy was watching; she said it was so nice that the two should be friends. She meant it, as far as it went, but no further. She would have to learn to mean it less and less; she would have to dislike and then to hate the idea of their being friends, if Jeannie's plan was to succeed. She would also have to hate one, anyhow, if not both, of the two whom she liked so much. The curtain had gone up on a tragic little farce. It was in order to avoid a tragedy, however, that the farce had been planned. It was in order to save Daisy that she was being sacrificed now.

Lady Nottingham took up Daisy's last question.

"Oh, yes, they have known each other for years," she said, helping the plan forward. "They met quite like old friends. I was completely out of it last night. We were just us three in the box, and I was the 'shadowy third.'"

Daisy stamped, figuratively speaking, on what was in her mind, and compelled her loyalty to triumph.

"I don't wonder at everybody simply loving Aunt Jeannie," she said. "We all do, don't we? But I don't love Lord Lindfield's motor. I do hope they will be in time for dinner. Otherwise the table is absolutely upset, and I shall have to settle it all over again. Isn't it rather inconsiderate of them, Aunt Alice? I think they ought to have caught their train, whether it was Brahms or not."

But the loyalty was an effort. Lady Nottingham felt that, and applauded the effort.

"Poor Daisy!" she said, speaking in these two words her unspoken thought. "It is too bad of them to give you more trouble."

"Oh, I don't mind just arranging the table again," said Daisy, quickly.

CHAPTER XII.

A rearrangement of the table proved to be necessary, since at half-past eight Lord Lindfield's motor had not yet been heard of. But in spite of the absentees, it was a hilarious party that sat down. Some had been on the river, some had strolled about the garden, and all were disposed to enjoy themselves immensely. Jim Crowfoot had not ceased talking at all, and showed at present not the slightest sign of doing so. He took Daisy in to dinner.

"They are probably sitting by the roadside," he said, "singing Brahms to each other, while the chauffeur lies underneath the car hammering it, with his feet just sticking out, and trying to screw the throttle into the waste-pipe of the carburetter. Why does nobody invent a motor car without a carburetter? It is always that which is at the root of the trouble. And the shades of evening will thicken, and they will sing louder and louder, as night draws on, to check their rising sensations of cold and hunger and fear, while the chauffeur swiftly and firmly reduces the car to scrap-iron. I think it is so interesting when somebody doesn't arrive. Their absence gives rise to so many pleasing conjectures. What are we going to do to-morrow, Miss Daisy?"

"Oh, nothing, I hope," said she. "Why? Do you want to do anything?"

"No, but if I was expected to do anything, I wished to know the worst at once. What I like best of all is to sit in a chair and not read. The chair ought to be placed at some railway station, and a succession of people should be provided to run by me with heavy bags in their hands just missing their trains. The next best thing to doing nothing yourself is to observe everybody else trying to do something, like catching trains, and not succeeding. My uncle once missed eight trains in one day, and then tried to commit suicide. But next day he caught nine trains and a motor 'bus, which reconciled him to living, which he is still doing."

"Are you sure he was your uncle?" asked Daisy.

"Not quite; but it is much better style to say a thing happened to your uncle than to confess that you made it up. If you make things up people expect you to write a novel or something, whereas nothing can be expected from you if you say it happened to your uncle. I haven't got any uncles. That is such a good thing; I can't be an anxiety to them. And nobody is an anxiety to me."

The dining-room looked towards the front of the house, and Daisy turned suddenly.

"Ah! surely that is the crunch of a motor on the gravel," she said. "I expect it is they."

That it was a motor was at once put beyond the region of doubt by a succession of loud hoots, and in a couple of minutes Jeannie appeared in the doorway.

"Dear Alice," she said, "I apologize most abjectly; at least, the motor apologizes. Lord Lindfield made it apologize just now at the top of its voice. Didn't you hear it? Don't scold us. We missed the train by about twenty minutes, as it is always best to do things thoroughly. Shall we dress, or may we come into dinner just as we are?"

Jeannie looked radiantly round while chairs and places were being laid for them, shaking hands with those nearest her, smiling at others, and kissing her hand across the table to Daisy. The swift movement—it had been extremely swift for the last ten miles after the car had got to work again—and the change from the cool night air into this warm bright room had brought the blood to her cheeks, and gave a wonderful sparkle and youthfulness to her face, and she sat down at the top of one of the sides of the table with Lord Lindfield between her and Alice.

"And we are so hungry," she said; "for the last half-hour we have talked of nothing but food. I couldn't look at the pink after-glow of the sunset because it reminded me of strawberry fool, and Lord Lindfield nearly burst into tears because there was a cloud shaped like a fish. And we had no tea, you see, because we were missing our train at tea-time."

Dinner went on its usual way after this, and Daisy succeeded in giving a less distracted attention to Jim Crowfoot, for up till their arrival she knew that she had really been thinking about them only. She still felt a little hurt that instead of coming down here early to-day Lord Lindfield had been prevented from doing that only by his subsequent engagement to take Aunt Jeannie to a concert; but very likely he had thought over his half promise to arrive early, and seen, which was indeed the case, that it was not quite a usual thing to do.

No doubt that was it; no doubt he would explain it to her afterwards, and Daisy settled in her own mind that she would at once admit the reasonableness of it, though she would let it appear that she was a little disappointed. And she was delighted that Aunt Jeannie liked him; she had said that before to Lady Nottingham, but it was truer now than when she had said it. For she had been conscious then of something in her own mind that did not agree with the speech; she had been glad that Aunt Jeannie liked him, but she would have been quite equally glad if she did not.

It was not quite a nice feeling; there was something in common between it and jealousy, and it had required a certain effort, which she had gladly made, to put it away from her. That she had done.

From where she sat she could just see him at the head of the table, side by side with Lady Nottingham; but she let herself look at him no more than she looked, with but casual glances, at any of the others. But it was very often that she heard, and allowed herself to listen for, that great boisterous laugh which contained so much enjoyment. Her rare glances in his direction, however, told her that it was Aunt Jeannie to whom he was talking, for after a word or two to Lady Nottingham just after he came in they had had no further conversation together. It was clear, then, that he liked Aunt Jeannie. That was a good thing also.

The door from the dining-room was at that end of the room at which he was sitting, and Daisy, on her way out, had to pass close to him. He had not finished his talk with her aunt even then, for they both stood by their chairs, she waiting till others had passed out. But as Daisy came up he saw her.

"Why, Miss Daisy," he said, "haven't seen or heard you all dinner-time. Been practising for a future incarnation as a mouse or some dumb animal? Well, this is jolly, isn't it? And Mrs. Halton's forgiven me for having a motor that breaks down, on condition of my getting one that doesn't."

"Daisy darling," said Aunt Jeannie, putting her arm round the girl's waist, "how are you? You must take my side. After having stuck for an hour on a perfectly flat road, is it unreasonable that I couple my forgiveness with a new car?—You shall have our ultimatum afterwards, Lord Lindfield. Daisy may make harder conditions than I, and if she does, I shall certainly adopt them. Now, do look bored pretty soon, and come out of the dining-room quickly. It is barbarous this separation of the sexes after dinner. You don't stop behind after breakfast to drink tea."

The others had passed out, and Daisy and Mrs. Halton brought up a rather detached rearguard. The rest had gone straight out of the house into the verandah, where they had had tea, for the night was exquisitely soft and warm, and they followed them there.

"Ah! such a concert, Daisy," said Jeannie. "I wish you could have been there. And such a ludicrous drive as we had. It is so pleasant meeting Tom Lindfield again; we were great friends a year or two ago, and I think we are great friends still. But, my dear, our drive! We went for the first hour well inside the four-miles-an-hour limit, and eventually stuck on a perfectly flat road. Then the chauffeur chauffed for an hour or two, and after that we came along a shade above the fifty-miles-an-hour limit. Our limitations were our limits throughout. And such nonsense as we talked!"

"Oh, do tell me," said Daisy. "Nonsense is the only thing I care to hear about."

"I couldn't. I can't remember anything. I only know I laughed quite enormously and causelessly. Ah, here they all are.—Alice, what a divine place, and how it has grown up? Like Daisy. I was telling her about my ridiculous drive with Lord Lindfield."

Jeannie sat down in a big basket-chair and became suddenly silent. She felt queerly tired; she felt also rather sick at heart, and looking at Daisy, she could not bear the thought of the trouble and disquietude she must bring to the girl whom she so loved. She had saddled herself with a load that already galled her, though she had barely taken it up, and even as she spoke of her ludicrous drive there came to her mind an aspect of it, namely, the purpose for which she had driven down with him, which was not ludicrous at all.

And here, in this starlit garden, with friends on all sides of her, it seemed an incredible thing that she had got to sow suspicion and discord. Trouble and sorrow seemed so remote, so utterly alien. Security and serenity had here their proper home; it was a place of pleasantness and friends and rest. She felt much inclined to yield to its influences, to put off the execution of her scheme, saying to herself that it was wiser to think over it again, and see if there was not, as surely there must be, some other possibility of detaching Daisy from the man whom it seemed certain she would otherwise marry, and whom it was quite impossible she should marry. Even now Daisy was standing near her, trusting her so implicitly, loving her so well. That love and trust, so intensely dear to her, she had to risk disturbing; indeed, it was scarcely a risk she ran, it was a certainty she courted.

However quietly and well she did her part it was impossible that Daisy should not see that she was encouraging Tom Lindfield, was using a woman's power of attraction to draw him towards her. True, Daisy had not as yet told her that she expected to marry him;

officially, as far as Daisy was concerned, she herself was ignorant of that. But supposing Daisy confided in her? There was nothing more likely. Within the next four-and-twenty hours Daisy would quite certainly see that her aunt was very intimate with Lord Lindfield. That very intimacy would encourage Daisy to tell her. Or, on the other hand, Lord Lindfield, while still thinking that she was only a very pleasant, sympathetic woman, might tell her his hopes with regard to Daisy. That was a very possible stage in the process of his detachment.

Yet she knew that personally she could make no better plan than that which she had already begun to carry out. She had thought over it, and thought over it, and one consideration remained paramount, namely, that Daisy must never know why this marriage was so unthinkably impossible. If he proposed to her, it seemed certain that she would accept him. In that case she would have to be told. Clearly, then, his proposal must be averted. She could find no other plan to avert that than the one she was pursuing, and already, partly to her relief, partly to an added sense of the meanness of her own rôle, she believed that his detachment would not be so difficult to manage. He had responded very quickly and readily to her advances; he had come to the concert with her and was delighted to miss the train, having told her also that he had "thought" of going down early to

Bray. He had said no more than that, and she had quite legitimately laughed at the idea of his spending the day alone with two girls, had professed herself as pleased to have upset so preposterous an arrangement. Yet this, too, though she was glad to have stopped it, added to her heart-sickness. He would not have made such an arrangement unless Daisy had allowed it. And if Daisy permitted him to come down to spend the day with her and Gladys, it surely implied that Daisy wanted very much to see him. But Lady Nottingham had told her that Daisy was not in love with him. That was still an anchor of consolation.

All this was no effort of consecutive thought which required to be reasoned out. It was all in front of her, spread out like a landscape, to be grasped in a moment. There was Victor, too....

Daisy moved a step nearer her chair.

"It's three days since you got back, Aunt Jeannie," she said, "and I haven't had a real word with you yet. May I come and talk to you this evening when we go up to bed? I have such heaps to say."

This was too dangerous. At any cost Jeannie wanted to avoid an intimate conversation with Daisy. She had her work to do, and she did not think she could go through with it if Daisy told her in her own dear voice what she already knew. She herself had to be a flirt, had to exhibit this man to Daisy in another light, to make her disgusted with him. That was a hard row to hoe; she did not want it made more difficult.

Luckily, even as Daisy spoke, an interruption came. The sound of men's voices sounded from an open door.

"My darling, how I long to talk to you," she said, "or, rather, to have you talk to me. But to-night, Daisy, I am so tired. When I can escape and go to my bedroom, I shall just tumble into bed. You look so well, dear, and so happy. You couldn't tell me anything nicer than that. Ah! here are the men. Let us multiply ourselves."

CHAPTER XIII.

Lord Lindfield had carried out Jeannie's instructions to the letter, and after the women had left the dining-room had relapsed into a state of supreme boredom. It had not been a difficult task; his boredom was quite genuine, for he did not in the least wish to talk to Victor Braithwaite or to listen to Jim Crowfoot, or pass the wine to two or three other men. He wanted to tell Daisy how impossible it had been to get down earlier in the day; he wanted also to tell Mrs. Halton what a jolly drive they had had together. It had been jolly; there was no question whatever about it. She had been so delightful, too, about the breakdown of that wretched motor car. Other women might have been annoyed, and audibly wondered when it was going to start again. But she had not been the least annoyed. She had said, "Oh, I hope it will take a long time to mend! Isn't it heavenly sitting by the roadside like tramps?"

They had sat like tramps for an hour or two. She did not look particularly like a tramp, for she had a huge fur cloak on at first, designed originally to defeat the cold wind occasioned by the speed at which they hoped to travel, which up till then had been about three miles an hour. This she had taken off, and sat on a rug taken from the disgraceful car, and treated the whole affair like a huge joke. There never was such a good comrade; if she had been a boy, out on a motor for the first time, she could not have adopted a franker air of amused enjoyment at these accidents of the road. They had made periodic visits to the car and the hammering chauffeur, and then the Great Hunger, about which she had already spoken, had begun. She had confessed to an awful inanition, and had suggested things to eat, till the fact that other people were already sitting down to dine, having had tea, became absolutely unbearable. Then suddenly she had stopped the nonsense and said, "I am so glad that this has happened. Being left in the Bath Road like this makes one know a man better, doesn't it? I always wanted to know you better. Oh, the compliment is ambiguous. I haven't told you yet whether you improve on acquaintance."

And then, just as they stopped at the door and the motor hooted its apologies, she turned to him.

"What a pity!" she had said. "I hate nice things coming to an end."

That particular nice thing had certainly come to an end, but he was firmly determined that there were a quantity of nice things not yet begun. He was genuinely attached to Daisy; he fully intended to ask her to be his wife, and contemplated, in case he was so fortunate as to obtain a "yes" from her, many serene and happy years. And, indeed, he was no coxcomb; he did not fancy that any girl he saw was willing to marry him if he wished to marry her, but at the same time he did not feel that it was in the least likely that Daisy would refuse him. And as he came out after dinner that night, after so successfully looking bored in the dining-room, he had not altered his mind in the least; his intentions were still all fully there. But that was no reason why he should not talk to Mrs. Halton. He was quite capable even of talking to her about Daisy.

It was then that the action of the tragic little farce really began. Daisy had heard the sound of his voice before they turned the corner of the house, and by design moved away from her aunt's side to the far end of the verandah, from where a path led down to the edge of the river. The verandah was well lit; there could be no question that when he came round the corner he would see her. There was no question, moreover, in her own mind, that he would join her.

Jeannie was sitting at the end of the verandah near to the corner round which they came. Victor Braithwaite stopped on one side of her chair, Lord Lindfield stopped on the other. The latter had looked up, and, Daisy felt sure, had seen her. Then, after a few minutes' chat, Daisy saw her aunt get out of her chair and heard her laugh.

"But I challenge you, Lord Lindfield," Daisy heard her say; "and, apart from all chivalrous instincts, if you don't accept my challenge it will be because you know you will be beaten. We will have a game of pool first, and then, when everybody else is tired, you and I will play a serious hundred. You probably think that because I am a woman I can't play games. Very well. I say to that, 'Let us put it to the proof.'—Mr. Braithwaite, come and play pool first, won't you?—Dear Alice, may we go and play pool? Is nobody else coming? Let us begin at once."

All this Daisy heard; and once again she saw Lord Lindfield look up towards the end of the verandah where she was standing, and then call some laughing reply after Mrs. Halton, who was already just vanishing indoors. For a couple of steps he followed her, then turned round and came up the verandah towards Daisy.

"Mrs. Halton has arranged a regular night of it, Miss Daisy," he said, "and has challenged me to a game of billiards in such a way that I can't refuse. We're going to have a game of pool first. Won't you come and take a hand? You and I will play Mrs. Halton and Braithwaite."

"Sides at pool?" asked Daisy.

"Why shouldn't we? But probably you think it's stupid to go indoors on such a night. So it is. I would much sooner stroll about or go on the river, but, you see, I can't help myself. Let's go in the punt to-morrow. Please keep a punt for you and me. Put a label on—'You and Me.'"

Daisy smiled. She would not have allowed that she needed cheering up at all, but it is a fact that this cheered her up.

"Yes, do let us spend all day on the river to-morrow," she said. "But you must go and play your pool now. I don't think I shall come in; it is so heavenly out here."

Lord Lindfield wavered; the girl looked enchantingly pretty. "Upon my word, so it is," he said; "and you look just like a summer evening yourself, Miss Daisy. Wonder if I could get some one to take my place at pool before I play a single with Mrs. Halton, and stop out here with you?"

Pleasant though the deed would have been to Daisy, his wish and his desire were more essential. She could without struggle forgo the pleasure of being with him, now that he had said that it was this that he preferred.

"But indeed you mustn't do anything of the kind," she said. "Aunt Jeannie wants you to play; she asked you. You must go in at once."

The fact that Mrs. Halton had carried off two men to the billiard-room left the rest of the party out of the square; but Daisy, quite willing to be the odd unit, strolled very contentedly out along the path that led to the river. The moon had not long risen and shone very large and low in the east, burning dimly and red through the heat haze and vapours from the Thames. The air was very windless, and the river lay like a sheet of grey steel at her feet, save where a little spreading feather of black ripple showed the course of some water-rat. Bats wheeled and dipped like some company of nocturnal swallows, pursuing their minute prey, and uttering their little staccato cries so high in the scale that none but the acute ear could hear them.

From the garden, as an occasional whisper of wind lifted the down-dropping leaves of aspen and ash, the air came laden with the scent of damp earth (for since sunset the gardeners had been busy) and the spilt fragrance of sleeping flowers. Or occasionally a little draught would draw from the river itself, and that to Daisy's nostril was of even a more admirable quality, for it smelt of cool running water and nought besides. On the far bank the mists lay in wisps and streamers above the low-lying meadow, and the dark bulk of cattle and horses loomed through them like rocks in a vaporous sea. But a fathom from the ground the air was dry and clear; it was but in a shallow sea that these rocks were submerged, and on this side of the river where Daisy walked the banking-up of the path to form a protection to the garden against the spring and winter floods raised her above these damp breathings of the fruitful earth, and she moved in the clearness and austerity of starshine and moonlight. And not her body only, but her mind and soul walked in a light that was very romantic and wonderful, and seemed somehow to be attuned to this pale mysterious flame of the moon that flooded the heavens.

All the dim, intense happiness she first experienced two nights before had blazed up within her into a conflagration, the nature of which there was no mistaking, while the dim and almost intenser doubts and miseries of two nights before she saw now to be but the shadows cast by the first kindling of the other light. Now, as it blazed higher and more triumphantly, the shadows vanished. And though her consciousness of this was so vivid and alert, self-consciousness was almost altogether banished. She no longer made plans for herself in the future, as she had always done till now, seeing herself as the mistress of a great house, and filling that position, as, indeed, she was fitted to do, so well, or seeing herself always kind, always pleasant, always ready to smile on her adorer. Nor did she even see herself as mother of his children. She lost sight of herself altogether just now, and saw him only, but in that different light in which he had appeared so suddenly, so disconcertingly, at the ball two nights ago.

And he had wished, had preferred to come out here with her rather than go indoors and play billiards. Daisy, in a sudden mood of that exquisite humbleness which goes with love, blushed with pleasure that it should be so, but told herself that it was an incredible thing. Yet so it was. He would sooner have come out here (for he had said it) and talked to this goose of a girl than be with anybody else, even Aunt Jeannie. Daisy wished she had told Aunt Jeannie on the afternoon of her arrival what was the state of things between her and Lord Lindfield, for it was really rather too much of a good thing that Aunt Jeannie (the darling) should all innocently monopolize him the whole afternoon, drive down with him alone (taking hours and hours over it), and as soon as dinner was over (at which meal she sat next him) take him away to play billiards. But she had let that opportunity slip, and though she had hoped to tell Jeannie about it to-night she would not be able, since her aunt had cried off a bedroom talk on the plea of tiredness.

And then, quite suddenly, a thought occurred to Daisy of the most disagreeable kind. Aunt Jeannie had been too tired to talk to her, had meant to slip away and tumble into bed as soon as possible, yet within five minutes of her having made that declaration she had engaged herself to play pool and to follow that up by having a single with Lord Lindfield—an odd programme for a woman who was so fatigued that she was going to slip away and go to bed as soon as possible.

Then, almost without pause, Daisy pulled herself together again, banging the door of her mind, so to speak, on that unpleasant thought, and refusing to give it entrance or to hold parley with it. There were fifty explanations, if explanations were required, but for a loyal friend they were not, and Daisy refused to think more of the matter. But all the time some small prying denizen of her subconscious mind was wondering what these explanations could possibly be.

This unpleasant little moment, though she had dealt with it as loyally and speedily as she could, had rather spoilt the moonlight saunter—or, at any rate, Daisy was afraid of other similar intrusions, and she went back to the house. There she found the whole party engaged, for the bridge tables had been made up, one in the far end of the billiard-room, one out on the verandah, while the remaining three were still at their pool. Without more than half-conscious intention, Daisy strolled on round the house, meaning to look in at the billiard-room.

She had meant to go into the room in the natural, ordinary way, entering by the long French window, which gave on to the path, and would be sure on this warm evening to be open. But she did not do that, and instead, paused opposite the window, but at some little distance from it, so that she herself was probably invisible to eyes looking from that bright light inside into the dusk in which she stood. She wanted, in fact, to see what was going on without being seen. She saw.

Aunt Jeannie and Lord Lindfield were standing together by the marking-board, talking about some point which might or might not have been connected with billiards. The pool apparently was over, for Victor Braithwaite had put down his cue and had strolled over to the bridge table. And at that moment Jeannie raised her hand and laid it, just for a second, on the sleeve of Lindfield's shirt, for he was coatless. The action was infinitesimal and momentary, but it looked rather intimate.

And then poor Daisy had once more to take herself in hand. Whatever polite name might be found for her present occupation (you could call it strolling in the garden or looking at the moon, if you chose), there was a very straightforward and not very polite name that could be found for it, and that was "spying." She discontinued it, and entered the billiard-room, whistling, like a proper person.

The usual thing happened, and everybody became so stupidly and obstinately unselfish that it looked as if there would be no more billiards at all.

Lord Lindfield, without pause, said: "By Jove! how lucky, Miss Daisy. You've come in the nick of time. Just finished our pool. Now you and Mrs. Halton shall play a single and I shall mark for you."

But it appeared also that if there was a thing Mrs. Halton really enjoyed doing it was marking for other people, and she insisted that Daisy and Lord Lindfield should have a game. Daisy, of course, was equally altruistic, firmly refused to interfere with their previous arrangement, and eventually, a rubber just coming to an end, cut into the bridge table in the far corner of the room.

The rubber was fairly rapid, but before the end of it a footman had appeared with the bed-time tray of soda and whisky and lemons, followed by another man with bedroom candles. Mrs. Beaumont, the only other woman in the room besides Daisy and Mrs. Halton, and who had been yawning in a strangled manner during the course of the last two hands, instantly took her candle and departed, and Daisy, with more deliberation, drank some soda-water and looked on at the game for a few minutes.

"Daisy dear," said Jeannie, "is it too dreadful and wicked and fast of me to go on playing? I don't care if it is. I must finish the game, and I'm going to win.—Oh, Lord Lindfield, what a fluke! Do you mean to say you are going to count it?"

"By Jove! yes; charge three for that.—Miss Daisy, your aunt's giving me an awful hiding! There, I've left them again!"

Jeannie, as a matter of fact, was what may be called a very decent country-house player, quite capable of making her twenty-five break more than once in the course of a game. She selected this moment to do it now, and from seventy-six ran out. The other men had strolled out on to the terrace, and Daisy, after congratulations, lit a couple of candles, one for herself, one for her aunt.

"I say, Mrs. Halton, we might have one more game," said Lord Lindfield; "it's only half-past ten. Couldn't sleep if I had to finish up with such a whacking."

Jeannie's eyes were a-sparkle with enjoyment and triumph.

"Have a game with Daisy," she said. "Let me rest on my laurels."

Daisy shook her head.

"Not to-night," she said. "I really would rather not. Do play again, Aunt Jeannie. I am going to bed; I am, really."

"Fifty, then, Lord Lindfield," said Jeannie.

Daisy went straight up to her room, still making an effort to banish the thought that Aunt Jeannie had said she was tired, and slowly the house grew quiet. The steps of men going to their rooms tapped along the polished boards of the corridor outside, with now and then the rustle of a dress. Then all was still, and she sat, half-undressed, with a book on her lap that she was not reading, while a couple more quarters chimed from the clock above the stables. At last came the sound of steps again outside; the tap of a rather heavy tread, and with it the rustle of a dress. Then came Lindfield's laugh, merry and unmistakable.

"Good-night, Mrs. Halton," he said. "I've had a perfectly ripping time! Never enjoyed a day more."

Apparently she had gone down the passage some way, for her voice sounded more distant.

"And I also," she said. "Good-night."

Then came the sound of two doors shutting.

CHAPTER XIV.

It was about half-past three in the afternoon of the next day, and house and garden alike wore a rather uncomfortable air of heat fatigue and somnolence. The blinds were down in all the windows that faced south and west, with the object, no doubt, of keeping them cool—a most desirable condition of things, but one, on the present occasion, but imperfectly realized. Nor were things much better to the east of the house, where ran the deep verandah in which they had sat and from which Daisy had strayed the evening before; for the heat came no longer from the honest and scorching rays of the sun, but through a thick blanket of grey cloud, which all morning had been gradually forming over and obscuring the sky. Southwards there was rather an ugly glare in the day, a tawny, coppery-coloured light that spread from low on the horizon, where clouds of thicker and more palpable texture were piled together—clouds with hard edges and angry lights in them. It was certain there was going to be a storm somewhere, and that would be no bad thing, for the air was horribly sultry, and quite distinctly needed clearing.

Daisy was always susceptible to atmospheric conditions, and she had gone upstairs after lunch to her room, on the plea, a fairly true one, of thunder-headache. Aunt Jeannie had been eager with sympathy, smelling-salts, and offers to read, but Daisy had quietly rejected all these, saying that it was merely a question of thunderstorm. When the storm broke she would be better; till then smelling-salts would not help her.

"It's quite darling of you, Aunt Jeannie," she had forced herself to say at the end, with a cordiality that was somewhat hard to put into her voice; "but, really, I would sooner be alone. It isn't a bad headache either— only just a thunder one."

There was a window-seat in her room, well lined with cushions, and looking over the river, and it was here that Daisy was rather uneasily reclining herself. She had first tried lying on her bed, but the room was too airless except close by the window to be tolerable. Partly that, partly (half an hour ago) the sound of voices outside, had made her come over here, and it was to see what was happening to those whom she had heard talking, as well as to get what air there was, that kept her here now.

A breath-holding immobility lay over river and garden; no quiver moved in the aspens or shook the leaf-clad towers of the elms and chestnuts. It was as if, instead of being clad in soft and sensitive foliage, they were cast in iron. No note of birds came from the bushes, no ripple broke the metallic hardness of the river, and the reflections of the loose-strife and tall grasses along its edges, and the clump of chestnuts on the little promontory at the corner of the garden, were as clear-cut and unwavering as if they had been enamelled on steel. There was no atmosphere in the day; no mist or haze, in spite of the heat, shrouded or melted the distances; the trees and house-roofs of Maidenhead a mile away seemed as if a stretched-out finger could be laid on them. They were of Noah's Ark size; it was only minuteness that showed their remoteness.

There was a punt underneath these chestnuts at the corner of the garden, partly concealed by the low sweep of the boughs. Half an hour ago Daisy had heard Aunt Jeannie's voice below her window saying, "Yes, with pleasure. But we shall be wise not to go far, as I am sure there will be a storm." It was at that that Daisy had left her bed and come across to the window-seat, to see with whom Aunt Jeannie was not going far. But before she had got there another voice had told her who it was. They had not gone far; they had gone about fifty yards from the boathouse.

She could see the lines of the punt among the leaves; there was a great pile of crimson cushions and a woman's figure dressed in grey. In front of it sat a man's figure in flannels, with shirt-sleeves rolled up to the elbows. Even as Daisy looked, Aunt Jeannie passed him a couple of cushions, and he too sat down on the floor of the punt, close to and facing her. Daisy had said her headache was not bad, and that it was only thunder-headache. Neither of these assertions was quite true. Her headache was bad, and it was not, in the main, thunder-headache at all; it was headache born of trouble and perplexity and struggle. She did not in the least understand what was happening.

She had got up early that morning and had gone out before breakfast. Very likely she was out of sorts, and a row on the river in the coolness of the day was exactly the right thing to correct morbid and suspicious impressions, which were founded, so she told herself, not on facts, but on her own bilious interpretation of facts. And, indeed, in the fresh dewy morning she found, when she went out, that her imagination, which had been fairly busy most of the night fitting together, like a Chinese puzzle, the rather disturbing events of the day before, had been riotous and sensational. Lord Lindfield, for instance, it was true, had not come down here early yesterday, as he had suggested, but had gone with Aunt Jeannie to a concert. Clearly his coming down alone to spend the day with two (especially one) girls in the country would have been highly unconventional, and he was very wise not to. So that was disposed of. They had missed their train and motored down instead, arriving half-way through dinner. What of that? Unless she was prepared to aver that there had been no breakdown, what was there to build on here? So that was disposed of. They had played two games of billiards together last night—the second fifty, so it appeared, had been doubled—but why not? Before each game Daisy had been asked if she would not play, and had refused. Then he had said, as they parted on the landing, that he had never enjoyed a day more. And what of that? Did not Daisy herself have "the most heavenly evening I have ever spent" about seven times a week?

Like the sensible girl she was, she took her trouble to bits in that early morning row, as one may take the mechanism of a clock to bits, and found there was something faulty in every individual piece of its working. Clearly, therefore, the whole thing, when pieced together again, could not reasonably be considered a reliable clock, since there was something wrong with every single piece of it. But—here was the trouble of it—it seemed to her, when reconstructed and made into one, to keep excellent time, to be thoroughly dependable. Yet, since all its pieces were wrong, she would not accept the whole, and, tossing it overboard, so to speak, settled down for a spell of demon-dispersing exercise. It was still only a little after seven. She had two clear hours to get rid of her blues—for they already had become substantial enough to take this depressing colour—before breakfast.

She had returned, it must be confessed, in far more equable spirits; physical exercise had disposed her to a broader and more out-of-door attitude, while her determined effort not to be suspicious and maliciously constructive had done more.

Of all people in the world Aunt Jeannie was the least mean or ignoble-minded, and Daisy told herself that she had been measuring her actions by a standard so crooked that it would not lie straight along them. There should be no more such attempts, and no more looking from the dark into windows to see unseen what people were doing inside. Flushed and exhilarated by her row, Daisy's cheeks burnt a shade brighter that moment at the thought that it was indeed she who had done that.

It was still half an hour to breakfast-time when she got back to the boat-house, but already the heat of the day was begun, and the smell of the damp coolness of the night dried up. She strolled along the outside of the thick hedge that faced the river, and then, turning the corner, saw in front of her, not twenty yards distant, two figures standing alone together. The woman's two hands clasped those of the man, holding them against her breast. She was speaking softly and eagerly, smiling into his face.

Quick as a lizard, Daisy popped back behind the hedge before either seemed to have seen her, and went swiftly to the house. But this was more inexplicable yet—for the two figures she had seen were those of Aunt Jeannie and Victor Braithwaite. There was no questioning the intimacy of their attitude. Yet here again she had seen something she had not been meant to see; she would be a lamentable creature if she let her mind dwell on it, or try to construct its meaning and significance. It was not for her. But if the man's figure had been Lord Lindfield's she would have been less surprised.

She had earned an inactive morning by her expedition before breakfast, and announced her set determination to go no further than the elm-trees beyond the rose-garden, and when arrived there to do nothing whatever. From the other side of the table Lord Lindfield rose at this.

"Jove, Miss Daisy," he said. "I've been wondering since I got up, what's the matter with me, and now I know it's the need of sitting under a tree and doing nothing. I'll join your party, if you'll let me. Is talking allowed?"

"Yes, but nobody need answer. I usually shan't."

Jim Crowfoot got up.

"I'm not sure if I shall come or not," he said. "I think not. I feel rather inclined for conversation to-day."

"Better not come then, old chap," said Lindfield. "There's not much conversation usually when I'm with you. I never get a word in. Nor anybody else."

It was impossible to take offence at even this, so pure and friendly was the chaff. It may be said to Jim's credit that he did not even attempt to do so.

"What am I to do, then?" he asked. "I can't converse alone.—Mrs. Halton, will you talk to me?"

"No, Mrs. Halton's going to write letters all the morning," said Lindfield. "She told me so."

Just for a second Daisy allowed herself to think "So he already knew that," but it was but momentary. This mood of drawing inferences from infinitesimal data in other people's conduct was altogether detestable; she must not allow herself to do it.

"Yes, I'm going to be a virtuous woman," said Aunt Jeannie.—"Alice dear, will you get a nice dog-chain and fasten me down to a writing-table till I swear to you that I have written to everybody who ever writes to me?"

"If you wish, but if I chain you down you sacrifice the fineness of your virtue. You make a virtue of necessity."

"No," said Jeannie, "I make a necessity of virtue. I shan't be able to get up. Or is it the same thing?"

"You're clearly going to make a morning of it," remarked Lindfield.

Jeannie sighed.

"An afternoon as well," she said, "If my recollection of the size of a certain packet neatly labelled 'Unanswered' is at all correct."

"Shouldn't make a packet of unanswered letters," said Lindfield. "I burn them. Then you can start afresh."

CHAPTER XV.

The next hour or two had fairly fulfilled the breakfast plans. Daisy, after the tiger accident to her parasol at the Zoo, had fallen back, for country use anyhow, on an immense scarlet contadina umbrella, and had planted herself and this under the elm-tree as soon as breakfast was over. Almost immediately after Lord Lindfield had followed her, with not quite so rigid an interpretation of idleness as Daisy, for she had brought absolutely nothing with her to occupy her hands or her mind, whereas he had a daily paper.

"Not a word or a sigh or a sneeze, Miss Daisy," he said, in a whisper, "or we shall be discovered. Not brought anything whatever with you? That's right. Just you yourself."

"You forget my parasol," said Daisy, "and it really isn't an insignificant affair."

"I know it isn't. I don't like it. It hides too much of you."

Daisy laughed.

"I suppose that means I have to put it down," she said.

"Well, I think it would be kind of you," he said. "You've been hiding yourself too much lately to my mind."

Daisy could not let this pass.

"Well, I like that," she said. "You threw me over all yesterday, which you said you were going to spend down here; you arrived with Aunt Jeannie in the middle of dinner, and played five thousand up with her afterwards."

"Yes, and when I do hope to catch a glimpse of you you hide yourself under a scarlet umbrella," he said. "That's better; thanks awfully."

Daisy furled the big umbrella, and threw it down on the grass. For the moment her mind was absolutely at peace again, and went back with a tremulous sense of happiness to the mood of the ball, so few evenings ago. And as she faced him, she thought again that it was a different man from the one she had known, and again saw that the difference was in herself.

"We had a great discussion, Mrs. Halton and I," he went on, "when we were sitting like wayside flowers near Ealing yesterday, as to whether people were nicer in the country or in town. I wonder which of us you will agree with."

"Oh, with Aunt Jeannie, I expect," said Daisy, not without challenge in her voice.

"H'm. That's a nasty one for me. Well, let's put it to the proof, anyhow. We agreed that some people are nicer in town and others in the country, but there we parted company."

"Ah, don't tell me," said Daisy. "Let me think."

She plucked a long grass stem and drew it through her teeth.

"The people one really likes and loves are nicer in the country," she said at length. "The people who just amuse you are nicer in town."

"Hurrah!" said he. "That's first-rate! It's what I said myself. Mrs. Halton wouldn't have any of that. She says that she herself is so much nicer in town that she refused to accept such a classification. Else it would mean that none of us liked her. But she stuck to the fact that none of us would like her so much down here."

Daisy considered this.

"How funny of Aunt Jeannie," she said. "I wonder—
—"

Then a whole collection of the things that poor
Daisy had tried to put away from her mind flashed into
it again, giving her a feeling of sickness and insecurity.
What did it all mean?

"I wonder what she meant?" she added, truthfully
enough.

"Don't know. Here she comes. By Jove! Miss Daisy,
how splendid she looks."

Aunt Jeannie certainly was looking her very best this
morning. She was walking hatless in the blaze of the sun,
and somehow the sunlight seemed not so much to shine
on her as to shine from her. Flowers, garden, river, sky,
sun, were all so much less splendid than she.

"I love this heat," she said, "and it saps my moral
nature and leaves me a happy animal with no sense of
responsibility. Daisy dear, you needn't answer. I won't
invade you for long. But I sat down at my table with all
the unanswered letters, I looked them through, and
determined not to answer one. I'm going to have a
holiday from being good. I've been good too long, I
think. The joy of virtue palls. But there ought to be

wind; there is sun and sky and water and all nice things, except wind. Can't you—what's the phrase?—can't you raise the wind, Lord Lindfield?"

Tom Lindfield clicked his finger and thumb together.

"Jove! Mrs. Halton," he said, "you always think of the right thing, or make me do so." He jumped up. "I'll order the motor at once," he said. "You and Miss Daisy and I, let's all go out for a run. Old Puffing Billy always goes well up to speed limit the day after he's broken down."

Daisy's effort with herself that morning on the river suddenly came to the limits of its energy. Once again she saw everything in that light which she had tried so hard to extinguish. And now there was more added, there were further features in the scene. Aunt Jeannie was too clever for her; with how natural an air she had come out and said that only wind was necessary to make the morning perfect; and how naturally and how unconsciously had he responded to that subtly conveyed suggestion, the very subtlety of which made him believe that he had thought of the plan himself. But outwardly Daisy still was mistress of herself; it was from the inside, not the outside, that her control was beginning to give way. She put up the red umbrella again.

"Thanks awfully, Lord Lindfield," she said, "but I can't think of the grilling roads and the dust without putting up my neat little parasol again. But you are too ingenious for words! Aunt Jeannie comes out here and demands wind, and you instantly think of the only plan of giving it her. No, for me the book of verses, or, rather, the newspaper, underneath the bough will last till lunchtime. Has anything happened?"

Daisy spoke in the lightest possible tone; it required a woman to hear that beneath the light words a troubled spirit spoke. And Jeannie was sick at heart at the success of her scheme. She had heard at breakfast how these two meant to spend their morning; she was aware that others knew of the situation which existed between them, and would surely avoid the elm-tree by the rose-garden like a plague-stricken spot, and so she had come out here on her hateful mission, interrupting and breaking up their dangerous companionship.

She had been prepared to go further than this—to ask, if necessary, point blank, for the use of his car, and hint at the pleasure of his company. Part of that had been spared her; he probably had no inkling of her design in coming out and demanding wind; indeed he thought he had thought of it himself. But Daisy knew.

The tragic farce had to preserve the tone required of public performances.

"Daisy dear, won't you come?" she asked. "Three is the best company of all, I think."

Daisy turned over a leaf of the paper rather too smartly for a public performance.

"Indeed, I think I won't, Aunt Jeannie," she said. "I had such a long row before breakfast. I feel frightfully disinclined to move."

And she waited to hear Lord Lindfield urge her to come. But he was already half-way towards the house. Daisy just raised her eyes, and saw him already distant, and she felt that which she had often heard of before, but passed over as unintelligible. Now she understood it, for her heart swelled.

Aunt Jeannie followed after a general remark or two, to which Daisy could scarcely reply. And after that more trials were in store, for Willie Carton brought his patient presence out under the elm-tree which had promised so well and performed so badly, and lay on the grass and pretended to read a book.

It was very stupid of him to come, so Daisy thought, and rather selfish. She had given him so firm an answer, and if he reopened the question again she was determined to speak even more plainly. But he did nothing of the kind, and Daisy, quieting down a little from the tumult of her private thoughts, began to feel a little compassionate.

She knew now, in some kind of way, what was going on inside him. She realized the nature of that which brought him out here, to pretend to read a book. He wanted to be near her. And there was something of the pathetic faithfulness of a dog about him—a dog that is beaten and repulsed but never falters, or can falter, in devotion to his master. She had begun to know what that unreasoning devotion meant.

"I know the compact of the elm-tree is not to talk or expect answers," said Willie quietly. "Don't let me disturb you."

Daisy looked up at him swiftly.

"But if I said that you do disturb me?" she said.

"Then I should go away," he said.

"Oh, Willie, you don't," she said.

"Right. Tell me when I do."

And then poor Daisy began to have a headache. It got worse, and before long she rose.

"What a beastly day," she said.

"It is rather," said he. "But it's all right here."

"It isn't all right anywhere," said Daisy. "I shall go indoors. I've got a headache."

"Wish I could take it," said he.

"Oh, don't be foolish. Thanks awfully; I know you mean it. But one can't take other people's burdens, you know. We are all saddled separately, and—and all we can do is to pretend we aren't saddled at all, and make grimaces and pretend to enjoy ourselves. Do pretend— we all pretend."

"Oh, I've been pretending a long time," said he.

Daisy's headache gave her a stab that was quite unsettling.

"Men always think about themselves," she remarked. "Don't answer. It is the elm-tree rule."

"I shall answer. Was your remark that men always think about themselves meant to apply to me? I only want to know."

Daisy had some little sense of justice left.

"No," she said. "I don't think it was."

———

The motorists came back very late for lunch, just as the evening before they had come back late for dinner.

———

Such was Daisy's morning; and she felt she had a perfect right to a headache. And with her headache she lay in the window-seat of her bedroom and watched the punt, with its crimson spots of cushions, unwaveringly reflected in the surface of the Thames. Above the sky grew darker with the approach of storm, and the light grew more coppery with the rising of that curious cloud out of the south. But still this dreadful clearness of air continued in spite of the growing darkness.

Maidenhead was still close and distinct, and closer and more distinct was the punt, where Aunt Jeannie handed Lindfield two crimson cushions. Then in that darkness below the chestnut-tree a match was struck, and he lit a cigarette, and dropped the still flaming vesta into the Thames. Then he shifted his position a little, and sat nearer to that other figure dressed in grey, whose arm was leaning over the side of the punt, and whose hand just dabbled in the water.

And then Daisy suddenly hid her face in the cushions of the window-seat and began to sob.

CHAPTER XVI.

Jeannie, as Daisy had heard, had advised that in view of the approaching storm they should not go far, and it was now about an hour since she and Tom Lindfield had, after this stipulation, gone down to the river. They had taken a punt, and pushed out from the hot, reeking boathouse that smelt strongly of the tar that was growing soft and viscous on its roof beneath the heat of the day, and slid down the backwater towards the river. The weeds here wanted cutting, and they wrapped themselves affectionately round the punt-pole, and dragged their green slender fingers along the bottom of the punt as if seeking to delay its passage. Then for a moment they had found a little coolness as they passed below the chestnut trees that extended their long boughs three-quarters of the way across the backwater, and Jeannie had said,—

"Lord Lindfield, you will certainly get very hot if you punt me up-stream, and we shall probably both get very wet before we get back. Let us stop here."

He had been by no means unwilling, and they had tied up.

"And sit down," she said; "out of these two thousand cushions I can spare you a few. There, on the bottom of the boat."

"I didn't suggest stopping," he said. "You mustn't be sarcastic afterwards over the immense expedition I took you."

"I promise not. I don't think I should ever be sarcastic to you, do you know? You would only laugh. The point of sarcasm is to give pain."

"And you don't want to give me pain? Hurrah!"

"Ah, I'm not sure that a little pain would not be rather good for you. I think you have almost too delightful a time. When did you last not enjoy yourself? And yet I don't know; perhaps you deserve it all. I am sure you give your friends a delightful time though you do have one yourself. Poor Daisy! I am afraid she isn't having a good time this afternoon; she has a headache. I offered sympathy and companionship, but she felt like being alone. Poor Daisy!"

Jeannie's voice suddenly died. She meant him to say something about Daisy, but for herself she felt as if she could not go on talking.

"I'm sorry," he said. "I thought she wasn't looking very brilliant. She should have come out with us for a run in the motor. Jove! it is hot even here. I think it was an excellent plan not to go any further; besides, I want to talk most awfully."

A week ago Jeannie had loathed the thought of this man even as, and for the same reason, she loathed the thought of Paris when she passed through it. But at the moment she did not loathe the thought of him at all, nor did she loathe him. She who so loved the sunshine and joy of life could not but like one who took so keen and boyish a pleasure in its pleasantness, and, boylike also, turned so uncompromising a back on all that was unpleasant or even puzzling.

He had no use for unpleasantness and no head for puzzles. From an intellectual point of view he might have been called stupid; but intellectual though Jeannie was, she never took her view of life or her estimate of people from that standpoint. Affection and simplicity and good-fellowship were things that seemed to matter to her much more.

From the human point of view, then, which does not concern itself with one's neighbour's intellectual qualities any more than it concerns itself with his morals, she had quickly grown to like this simple, pleasant man, who had so good an appetite for the joys of life. And her liking for him made her task far more difficult and far more repulsive to her than she had anticipated.

She had thought that as far as he was concerned she would find it perfectly easy to be ruthless, steeling herself to it by the memory of Diana. That memory had not in the least faded, but there had come into the foreground of her life this liking and sympathy for the man who she hoped was to be her victim.

It made what she was doing doubly odious to her, and yet, think and puzzle as she might, she could devise no plan but this, which, if it succeeded, would spare Daisy the knowledge that she herself had promised Diana to spare her.

As far as things had gone, she was fairly content with what she had accomplished. It was all horrible to her, but the plan was working quite well. He had scarcely seen Daisy since they had come down here, while he had seldom been out of her own company, and it was clear to Mrs. Halton that Daisy was certainly beginning to be puzzled, and, poor child, was beginning to feel hurt and slighted.

But there had been as yet no more than a beginning made; Lord Lindfield would have to be far more taken up with herself than he was now, and Daisy, poor dear, would have to be far more deeply wounded and hurt before the thing was accomplished. And already Mrs. Halton felt sick at heart about it all. Yet till a better plan could be thought of she had not to set her teeth, but to smile her best, and flirt, flirt, flirt.

There was but one bright spot in the whole affair, and that the few words which she had had with Victor early that morning before breakfast. She had asked him, not pointedly, but in a general way arising out of their talk, what he would think if in some way she completely puzzled him, and acted in a manner that was incomprehensible. And he had laughed.

"Why, my darling, what an easy question," he said. "I should know that there was something behind I didn't understand. I should wait for you to tell me about it."

"And if I never told you about it?" asked Jeannie.

"Then, dear, I should know you had some good reason for that. But I should never ask you, I think, and I know I should never cease to trust you or forget that we are—well, you and me."

That was wine to her.

CHAPTER XVII.

But she liked Lindfield; that made her task so much harder. It was shameful to treat a man like this, and yet—and yet there was still the memory of that dreadful gilded house in Paris and the dying voice of Diana.

So once more, and not for the last time, she settled down to the task that was so odious—odious because she liked him.

"We shall quarrel, then, I am afraid," she said, "because I want to talk too. We both want to talk—I to you, you to me."

He leant over her a moment, since the punt-pole had to be grounded at the stern of the boat, for he had tied the chain in the bow to an unearthed root of the tree. She leant a little sideways away from him, and this was done. It was then she gave him the few cushions out of the two thousand.

"Have you got anything very special to say?" she asked. "Because I have, and so I shall begin. Yet I don't know if it is special, except that between friends everything seems to be special."

Again Jeannie could not get on for a moment, but she proceeded without notable pause.

"The difference between friends and acquaintances is so enormous," she said, "and yet so many people confuse the two. One may meet another person a hundred times and be only an acquaintance; one may meet a person once and be a friend in a minute. Perhaps it is not the same with men. I don't think a man recognizes those who are going to be or are capable of being his friends at the first glance, whereas a woman does. She feels it to the end of her finger-tips."

Jeannie gave a quick glance at him, and saw that he was listening with considerable attention. She gave a little sigh, and clasped her hands behind her head.

"What an uneconomical world it is," she said, "and what a lot of affection and emotion Nature allows to run to waste. A man sees in some woman the one quality, the one character that he is for ever seeking; he sees that she is in some way the complement of himself, and perhaps the woman merely dislikes him. Or it may happen the other way round. What a waste of noble stuff that means. All his affection is poured away like a stream losing itself in the desert. It does seem a pity."

"Jove! yes, and I never thought of that," he said. "There must be a lot of that going on. So much, perhaps, that some day the desert will get quite damp, and then won't it cease to be a desert?"

She looked at him rather longer, letting her eyes rest on his.

"That is a much more hopeful solution," she said. "Perhaps it doesn't all go to waste. Or shall we say that Nature never throws things away, but puts all these odds and ends of affection in the stock-pot to make soup. But they will make soup for other people. Ah! there was lightning far off. The storm is beginning."

They waited in silence, till a long, drowsy peal of thunder answered.

"Oh, it is miles away yet," he said.

Jeannie arranged her cushions more comfortably. "And yet I rather like Nature's uneconomical habits," she said, "if we settle she is a spendthrift. There is something rather royal and large-handed about it. She is just the same in physical affairs. I saw in some snippety paper the other day that the amount of electricity discharged in a good thunderstorm would be sufficient to light every house in London for five hours, or run all the trains on all the tubes for about the same time. I should think you are rather spendthrift, too, Lord Lindfield."

He laughed.

"I? Oh, yes. I pour out gallons of affection in all directions. Always have."

Again Jeannie smiled at him.

"Ah, I like that," she said, softly. "And we won't think it goes to waste. It would be too sad. Go on, tell me about your pouring it out in all directions. I should like to hear about it."

Jeannie hated herself as she spoke; she was using all her woman's charm to draw him on, and—a thing which he could not follow, though she knew it well—she was using lightness of touch so that he should not see how much she was in earnest. She had used, too, that sacred name of friendship to encourage him to draw nearer her, for no man could listen to what she had been saying without reading into it some directly personal meaning; clearly the friendship she spoke of concerned him and her, for no woman talks to a man about friendship purely in the abstract unless she is his grandmother. And she was not; nobody could be less like a grandmother, as she sat there, in the full beauty of her thirty years and her ripened womanhood.

She was beautiful, and she knew it; she had charm, she was alone on this hot thundery day with him in the punt. Also she meant to use all power that was hers. The plan was to detach him from the girl, and the manner of his detachment was the attachment to her. Daisy must be shown how light were his attachments.

Indeed, the handicap of years did not seem so heavy now. She was perfectly well aware that men looked at her as she went by, and turned their heads after she had passed. And this hot, sweltering day, she knew, suited her and the ripe rather Southern beauty of her face, though in others it might only be productive of headache or fatigue. Indeed, it was little wonder that her plan had made so promising a beginning.

He moved again a little nearer her, clasping his knees in his hands.

"You've talked about friends," he said, "and you are encouraging me to talk about them. It's a jolly word; it means such a jolly thing. And I'm beginning to hope I have found one in this last day or two."

There was no mistaking this, nor was there any use in her pretending not to know what he meant; indeed, it was worse than useless, for it was for this she had been working. There was no touch or hint of passion in his voice; he was speaking of friends as a boy might speak. And she liked him.

She held out her hand with a charming frankness of gesture.

"That is a very good hearing," she said. "I congratulate you. And, Lord Lindfield, it isn't only you I congratulate; I congratulate myself most heartily."

He unclasped his knees and took her hand in both his.

"Thanks, most awfully," he said.

"Friends don't thank each other," she said. "One only thanks people who don't matter. Now go on. I have been doing all the talking these last two days. It is your turn; I want to know much more about you."

"I expect you won't like it."

"I must be the judge of that. I am willing to risk it."

"Well, I told you I wanted to talk most awfully," he said, "and now you've made it so much easier. I expect you know a certain amount about me, as it is. I've had a tremendously good time all my life. People have been very kind to me always. I expect they've been too kind. It's all been so confoundedly pleasant, I have let the years go by without ever thinking of settling down. But there's an awful lot to be said for it. And all my life—I'm thirty-eight already—I've shirked every responsibility under the sun."

Jeannie had a sudden sense that in spite of the promising beginning which she had half prided herself on and half loathed herself for, things were going quite completely wrong, and that she had as yet accomplished nothing whatever. It was but a momentary impression, and she had no time to reflect on or examine it, since she had to do her part in this sealed compact of friendship. But she did it with an uncourageous heart.

She laughed.

"I can't console you over that," she said, "or tell you that you do yourself an injustice, because I have always regarded you as the very type of the delectable and untrammelled life. You don't conform to the English standard, you know, and I expect you have no more acquaintance with your Wiltshire estates and all your people there than you have with the House of Lords. Have you ever taken your seat, by the way? No, I thought not. But, after all, if you don't know the House of Lords, you know London pretty well, and—and Paris."

He did not smile now, but looked at her gravely.

"Yes, worse luck," he said.

Jeannie nodded at him.

"Well, well," she said, quietly. "Never mind that now. You were speaking of settling down. Go on about that."

"One doesn't settle down alone," he said.

And then she knew that, so far, her plan had been a dead failure. His attitude towards her was perfectly clear; they were friends, and as friends should do, he was confiding in her, seeking from her the sympathy and counsel of a friend.

"You mean to marry, then?" she asked.

"I hope to marry."

Once again the lightning flickered in the sky, and the thunder gave a far more immediate response. That big coppery cloud which had been low on the horizon had spread upwards over the heavens with astonishing speed, and even as the thunder crackled a few big drops of rain splashed on the river outside their shelter under the chestnuts. The storm was quickly coming closer, and a big tree, as Jeannie remembered, is not a very desirable neighbourhood under the circumstances.

"We had better get home," she said. "There is going to be a storm."

He jumped up at once, loosed the chain, and with a few swift strokes took them back into the boathouse. There was no time just then for further conversation, and Jeannie, at any rate, did not wish for it. But it was as she had feared. All that she had done hitherto was nothing; the calamity she wished to avert had not yet been averted.

One thing only she had gained at present, the footing of a friend. Already, she was sure, he valued that, and on that she would have to build. But it was a precarious task; she could not see her way yet. Only she knew that such friendship as she had already formed with him was not enough. He was not detached from

Daisy yet. For the last forty-eight hours, it is true, he had almost completely left her alone, but that was not enough. He still intended to marry her.

Jeannie went straight to her room on gaining the house, under pretence of changing her dress, which even in those few yards across from the boathouse had got wet with the first rain of the storm. But she wanted not that so much as to sit by herself and think. Matters were not so easy as she had hoped, for she knew now that she had let herself believe that by the mere formation of a friendship with her, she could lead him away from Daisy. And now, for the first time, she saw how futile such a hope had been. He could, in the pleasure of this new friendship, be somewhat markedly inattentive to Daisy for a day or two, but it could not permanently detach him. She must seem to offer something more than mere friendship.

That he was seriously in love with Daisy she did not wholly believe, but he meant to marry her; he meant, anyhow, to ask her to marry him, and Alice, who knew better than she what Daisy felt, was sure that Daisy would accept him. But something more than a mere flirtation was required; matters, she saw now, had to go deeper than that. She must make herself essential to him, and then, when he knew that she was essential, she would have to turn her back on him. It was not a pretty rôle.

There came a gentle tap at the door, and Daisy entered.

"Ah! you have come in, Aunt Jeannie," she said. "Did you get caught in the storm?"

"Not to speak of. We did not go far. Lord Lindfield offered to take me up to Maidenhead, but, as a matter of fact, we went to the corner of the backwater. Oh, I promised not to laugh at him for the immensity of the expedition, because it was I who proposed stopping under the chestnuts. How charming he is, Daisy! And how is the headache?"

"Rather brilliant still, but it will get better. Aunt Jeannie, how quickly you make friends with people."

There was something tearing to Jeannie's tender heart about this. Daisy looked so white and tired, and so helpless, she who was usually a perfect well-spring of high spirits and enjoyment. Jeannie longed to take that dear head in her hands and kiss its trouble away, but it was just that which she could not do. This trouble could not be kissed away; it had to be burnt away—by a hand, too, that seemed unconscious of its cruel work.

"With him, do you mean?" she asked lightly. "You can scarcely say I have only now been making friends with him. I saw a good deal of him at one time; in fact, he was rather devoted to me. But my eagle eye sees no sign of a return of it. Does yours?"

The room was very dark with the blackness of the sky outside, and Jeannie could see Daisy but indistinctly. Then with a wicked flare of lightning it leaped into light, and the thunder rattled round the eaves. But in that moment's flash Jeannie saw Daisy's face again, mute, white, and appealing, and it was intolerable to her. Besides, anything was better and less dangerous than a *tête-à-tête* with Daisy. At any moment she might tell her about Lord Lindfield and the offer she expected. That would make her part infinitely worse to play; it would make it impossible. At present, anyhow, so far as Daisy knew, she was ignorant of it all.

She jumped at the appalling racket overhead.

"Oh, I hate thunder—I hate thunder," she said. "Let us come downstairs, Daisy, where there are people. Besides, it is tea-time, is it not? Let us go down. I came straight to my room, and Lord Lindfield, I think, went to his. Alice will be anxious if she thinks we are still out.

Listen to the rain. How it will beat the flowers down! Come, dear."

"I have hardly had a word with you since you came back, Aunt Jeannie," said Daisy.

"I know, dear, but in a house full of people what can one expect? We must have a great talk when we get back to London. Every moment seems occupied here. Dear child, I hope your headache will be better soon. Will you not go and lie down? Or shall I tell Alice you are not well, and won't you have a little dinner quietly in your room by yourself? No? Let us go down, then."

CHAPTER XVIII.

The storm was violent for an hour or two, but before sunset it had moved away again, and a half-hour of sunshine, washed, clean sunshine, preceded sunset. But somehow the storm had not done its proper work; it had scolded and roared and wept, but it had not quite got the trouble out of the air. There was more to come.

The same sense that there was more to come invaded the spirits of Lady Nottingham's guests. She herself was a little distraite, Daisy's headache had left her rather white and tired, Gladys lamented the wreck of the garden, and there was not much life about. Then after dinner it clouded over again, the clouds regathered, lightning began to wink remotely and thunder to grumble, and even Mrs. Halton, whom the sultry heat had so invigorated, according to her own account, that afternoon, was inclined to join in the rather early move to bed. Also, the next day was Sunday, and Sunday was not particularly wanted. The fact of it was felt to be a little depressing, and nobody quite knew what was the matter with everybody else.

It is a fact that in every gathering of friends and acquaintances there is some one person who makes *la pluie et le beau temps*, and in this party it was emphatically Jeannie Halton who arranged the weather. The spirits of every person are, to a certain extent, infectious, but the spirits of some few people run through a house like influenza, and there was no doubt that she had, all the evening, been in a rather piano mood. She had not, of course, committed the unpardonable social crime of showing that she was depressed, but she had been a little retrospective, and tended to "remember how" in general conversation, rather than to "hope that."

But it must not be supposed that she had behaved in any way outside the lines of normal social intercourse. She had, for instance, just gone out into the garden after dinner with Lord Lindfield, and had quoted the line, "In the darkness thick and hot." It was apt enough and harmless enough, but it had vaguely made him feel that something was a little wrong. Then she had made him and Daisy play billiards together, while she marked for them. She marked with weary accuracy, and said, "Oh, what a beautiful stroke" rather too often to make it credible that she always meant it. And with the rest of the women she had gone up to bed rather early.

Tom Lindfield, on the other hand, though he did not feel at all inclined to go to bed early, felt that there was trouble somewhere. He could not date it in the least, nor could he put his finger on the moment when trouble began. Or could he? He asked himself that question several times. Jeannie had been so pleasant and so good a comrade till they had gone out in the punt. Then came the compact of friendship, and somehow at once almost she seemed to slip away from him. He had wanted to tell her much more, to tell her even how in Paris he had been desperately in love, and that what he felt now for Daisy was not that. Somehow that woman in Paris reminded him of Daisy, and yet what two women could be more different than these! She had an apartment in the Rue Chalgrin. It was very much gilded, and yet very simple.

That did not occupy him much. What occupied him so much more was that till the storm had begun, till he and Jeannie had run hurriedly to the house, he had found such an extreme content in her society. She had been—for these last thirty hours or so—such an admirable comrade. There was the Brahms concert, the ridiculous motor-drive, the evening at billiards, the morning in the motor, the afternoon in the punt. Then quite suddenly she had seemed to shut up, to enclose herself from him. Yet some little spirit of companionship had escaped her again, when she quoted the line, "In the darkness thick and hot." And then, after that, she had walked back to the house, made him play billiards with

Daisy, and had gone upstairs at the earliest possible opportunity.

Nobody with the slightest prospect of winning his case could have accused Tom Lindfield of being sensitive in his perceptions, but nobody without the certainty of losing it could have accused him of not being fairly sound in his conclusions. What had happened to Mrs. Halton to make her so different to him (and, for that matter, to everybody else) since four o'clock that afternoon he did not try to decide, since he had no means of knowing.

But what he did know was that this was a woman of enchanting moods. At one time she was good comrade, then she was friend, then for some reason she was some sort of shadow of these excellent things. They were there, but they were obscured by something else. And that obscuration rendered her the more enchanting. He did not understand her; she was away somewhere beyond him, and he longed to follow her.

All his life women had been to him the most delectable of riddles, and his expressed desire to marry and settle down was perhaps only another statement of the fact that he longed to solve one example of the riddle, one form in which it was presented to him. He felt now that he wished he had married years ago, that he had already become quiet and domesticated. There was a time for youth's fiery passions, its ecstatic uncontent, and there was also most assuredly a time when those fevers should cease.

He had so repeatedly told himself that it was time they should cease for him, that of late he had come to believe it. He believed it still, and it was for that reason that he had determined to settle down, to choose, as he had done in his own mind, this pretty and charming girl, much younger than himself, as was right, and ask her to settle down with him.

He was not in love with her in any absorbed or tumultuous way, but he meant to do his best to make her happy, and looked forward to being immensely happy himself. All that had seemed very right and reasonable and satisfactory, but to-night, in some way, the mirror of his future tranquillity was disturbed; it was as if little sudden puffs of wind, like those that rustled every now and then through "the darkness thick and hot" outside, ruffled and broke its surface, making it dim and full of shattered images that seemed to have swum up from below.

Was it that once again he was beginning to fall in love with Daisy in the old passionate way? But at that moment he was aware that he was not thinking about Daisy at all.

All this passed very rapidly through his mind; it was no effort of conscious or reasoned thought, but more as if without volition of his own these pictures had been drawn across his brain, as he stood in the hall while the rustling procession of women went upstairs. And with their going, he became aware that the rest of the evening was likely to be rather boring.

It was still not after half-past ten, an hour impossible to go to bed at, impossible, anyhow, to go to sleep at, and he fancied that his own company and his own thoughts were not likely to be very comfortable or very profitable. He did not want to think; he wanted the hours to pass as quickly and unreflectingly as possible until it was morning again. No doubt then things would present themselves in a more normal light. Certainly the events of the day had proved rather exciting and unsettling, or, to be perfectly honest, Jeannie had somehow unsettled him. How quickly their friendship had sprung up! And what had happened then? She seemed to have left him altogether, glided away from him.

He strolled back into the billiard-room, where he would find company of some sort, but there already the hour of yawns and fitful conversation had begun, and first one and then another man nodded good-night and left the room. Jim Crowfoot, however, who hated going to bed as much as he disliked getting up, had a brilliant cargo of conversation on board, which he proceeded to unload. The two knew each other well, and when they were left alone conversation rapidly became intimate.

"Thunderstorms always are simultaneous with sombreness," he said, "and I sometimes wonder whether it is our sombreness that produces the storm or the storm that produces sombreness. Every one has been sombre to-day, except, perhaps, you, Tom, and the merry widow."

"Are you referring to Mrs. Halton?"

"I don't know of any other. Lady Nottingham isn't merry. I can't think how you manage to produce so much impression with so little material. I have to talk all the time to produce an impression at all, and then it is usually an unfortunate one."

"I think your description of Mrs. Halton as the merry widow is a particularly unfortunate one," remarked Lindfield.

"You guessed whom I meant," said Jim.

"I know. It was characteristic of you if not of her. You always see people in—in caricature. Besides, I thought Mrs. Halton was anything but merry."

"You should know best."

"Why?"

"Because you have spent the entire day with her, chiefly *tête-à-tête*. Also yesterday."

Tom Lindfield was apparently not in a very genial frame of mind to-night. He let this remark pass in silence, and then went back to what Jim had previously said.

"You always talk a good lot of rot, old chap," he said, "and I want to know if you were talking rot when you said something about my producing an impression with little material. It sounds pretty good rot, but if you meant something by it, I wish you would tell me what it was. Does it have any special application?"

"Yes, certainly. I referred to your 'Veni, vidi, vici' with Mrs. Halton. You laid firm hold of her yesterday, and have not let her go since. I don't imply that she has wanted to go."

Jim, in spite of the large quantities of outrageous nonsense which he often talked, had a very fair allowance of brains, and when he chose to talk sense was worth listening to. So, at any rate, Tom Lindfield thought now.

"I wish you'd go on," he said, "and just tell me all that is in your mind."

"By all means, if you promise not to knock me down or anything. It's just this—that we've all been asking ourselves, 'Is it to be the aunt or the niece?'"

"And who has been asking themselves that?" asked Lindfield.

"Oh, everybody except, perhaps, Braithwaite and poor wandering Willie. Mrs. Beaumont and Lady Sybil were hard at it when you and Mrs. Halton strolled out after dinner. They tore Mrs. Halton open as you tear open a—a registered envelope. With the same greed, you understand."

"Cats!" remarked Lindfield.

"Oh, yes. But I like to hear them 'meaow.' Braithwaite didn't; he listened to just one remark and then went away looking black."

"What has he got to do with it?" asked Tom.

"Oh, he's great friends with the M. W.," said Jim, "and he is one of those nice old-fashioned people who never talk evil of people behind their backs. But where are you to talk evil of people except behind their backs? That's what I want to know. You can't do it in front of their faces, as it would not be polite."

"Don't be epigrammatic, there's a good fellow," said Tom. "It only confuses me."

"Well, you've confused us. You were supposed to be walking out, so to speak, with Miss Daisy. Instead of which you leave her completely alone, and walk out all the time with Mrs. Halton. Oh, I don't deny that she is running after you. She is; at least, so the cats said. It's confusing, you know; I don't think any one knows where we all are."

Lindfield took a turn or two up and down the room, took up a cue, and slapped the red ball into a pocket.

"I'm sure I don't know where I am," he said, "but I expect we shall all be in the deuce of a mess before long. About Mrs. Halton running after me, that is absolutely all rot. What brutes women are to each other! And they say, to use your expression, that I've been walking out with Miss Daisy?"

"It has been supposed that you were going to ask her to marry you."

Lindfield sent one of the white balls after the red.

"And they weren't far wrong," he said. "Well, I shall go to bed, Jim. Your conversation is too sensational."

"Good-night. Mind you let me know when you have made up your mind," said Jim.

CHAPTER XIX.

It was this certainty that he had got to make up his mind, whereas till to-day he had believed that his mind was made up, that Lindfield carried upstairs with his bedroom candle. But, unlike that useful article, which could be put out at will, the question refused to be put out, and burnt with a disconcerting and gem-like clearness. It was perfectly true, and he confessed it to himself, that for the last two days he had distinctly preferred to cultivate this wonderful quick-growing friendship which had shot up between him and Jeannie, rather than bring things to a head with Daisy.

He had meant while down here to ask her to marry him; now, if he looked that intention in the face, he was aware that though it was still there (even as he had begun to tell Mrs. Halton that afternoon), it had moved away from the immediate foreground, and stood waiting at a further distance. The cats and Jim Crowfoot, he told himself with some impatience, were altogether at fault when they so charmingly said that he had to make up his mind between aunt and niece. It was not that at all; the only question with which the making up of his mind was concerned was whether he was going to ask Daisy now, to-morrow, to be his wife. And the moment he asked himself that question it was already answered. But that he did not know.

As always, he was quite honest with himself, and proceeded ruthlessly to find out what had occasioned the postponement of his intention. That was not hard to answer; the answer had already been indirectly given. It was the enchantment of this new friendship which had forced itself into the foreground.

That friendship, however, was now agreed upon and ratified, and the postponed intention should come forward again. But these last few hours had made him feel uncertain about that friendship. There was no use in denying it; she had been quite different since they came in from the punt. How maddening and how intoxicating women were! How they forced you to wonder and speculate about them, to work your brain into a fever with guessing what was going on in theirs.

He turned over in bed with his face to the wall, and shut his eyes with the firm and laudable intention of not bothering any more about it, but of letting sleep bring counsel. He did intend to ask Daisy to marry him, but he was not quite certain when he should do so. And then there outlined itself behind the darkness of his closed lids Jeannie's face, with its great dark eyes, its mass of hair growing low on the forehead, the witchery of its smiling mouth.

So perhaps the cats and Jim Crowfoot, though a little "previous," were not so wrong about the reality of the question on which he must make up his mind.

Jeannie announced her intention of going to church next morning at breakfast, and Victor Braithwaite, who was sitting by her, professed similar ecclesiastical leanings. Jeannie had apparently completely recovered from the piano mood of the evening before, and commented severely on the Sunday habits of this Christian country. She personally taxed every one who had at present come down with having had no intention whatever of going to church, and her accusations appeared particularly well founded. In the middle of this Lord Lindfield entered.

"Good-morning, Lord Lindfield," said Alice. "We are all catching it hot this morning from Jeannie, who has been accusing us by name and individually of being heathens."

"Worse than heathens," said Jeannie, briskly.—"Oh, good-morning, Lord Lindfield. I didn't see you.—Worse than heathens, because heathens don't know any better. Alice, you must come. You are a landlady of Bray, and should set an example."

"But it is so hot," said Alice, "and I don't take out the carriage on Sunday. I like to give the coachman an— an opportunity of going to church."

"You give him fifty-two every year," said Jeannie.

"The motor is eating its head off," remarked Lindfield. "I'll drive you. Do come with me, Mrs. Halton."

"Oh, thanks, no. I'll walk," she said. "Mr. Braithwaite is coming with me."

Jeannie rose as she spoke, and went out through the French window into the garden.

"Half-past ten, then, Mr. Braithwaite," she said.

Lindfield helped himself to some dish on the side-table.

"Can't stand being called a heathen," he said. "I shall go to church too."

Victor soon strolled out after Jeannie.

"Hang it all, Jeannie!" he said. "I want to go to church with you, and now Tom Lindfield says he is coming. Considering how much—oh, well, never mind."

Jeannie looked hastily round, found they had the garden to themselves, and took his arm.

"How much he has seen of me, and how little you have," she said.

"Quite correct. But it wasn't a difficult guess."

"No. We will be cunning, Victor. I said half-past ten quite loud, didn't I? Let us meet in the manner of conspirators at the garden-gate at a quarter-past."

They turned towards the house again, and Jeannie detached her arm from his.

"Remember your promise, dear," she said. "I am I, and I am yours. Never doubt that."

All that day there was no possible cause for his doubting it. The conspirator-plan succeeded to admiration, and Lord Lindfield and Daisy, with a somewhat faint-intentioned Gladys, had waited in the hall till a quarter to eleven. Then it was discovered that Jeannie had not been seen in the house since ten, and

Gladys, victorious over her faint intentions, had stopped at home, while Daisy and Lord Lindfield walked rapidly to church, arriving there in the middle of the psalms.

Jeannie had been gaily apologetic afterwards. She had not heard at breakfast that anybody except herself and Mr. Braithwaite meant to go to church, and, coming home, she paired herself off with Daisy. At lunch again there were, when she appeared, two vacant places, one between Willie Carton and one of the cats, the other next Lord Lindfield. She walked quietly round the table to take the first of these, instead of going to the nearest chair.

For the afternoon there were several possibilities. Jeannie, appealed to, said she would like to go up to Boulter's Lock and see the Ascot Sunday crowd. That, it appeared, was very easy of management, as Lord Lindfield would punt her up.

"That will be delightful," said Jeannie. "Daisy dear, I haven't simply set eyes on you. Do let us go up together, and Lord Lindfield will punt us. We will be the blest pair of sirens, of extraordinarily diverse age, and he shall give the apple of discord to one of us. If he gives it you I shall never speak to you again.—Lord Lindfield, will you take us up?"

"I shall have two apples," said he.

"Then Daisy and I will each of us want both."

This had been the last of the arrangements, and it was like Mrs. Halton, such was the opinion of the cats, to manage things like that. There could be no doubt that when the launch and the Noah's Ark and the punt met below Boulter's, it would be found that Daisy had another convenient headache.

The three vessels met there. But on the punt were Lord Lindfield and Daisy all alone. Mrs. Halton, it seemed, had stopped at home. There was no explanation; she had simply not come, preferring not to.

Nobody could understand, least of all Lord Lindfield. She had swum further away.

But Daisy had not had a very amusing time. Punting appeared to monopolize the attention of the punter.

CHAPTER XX.

All that day and throughout the greater part of the next Jeannie kept up with chill politeness and composure this attitude towards Lord Lindfield, which he, at any rate, found maddening. What made it the more maddening was that to all the rest of the party she behaved with that eager geniality which was so characteristic of her. Only when he was there, and when he addressed her directly, something would come over her manner that can only be compared to the forming of a film of ice over a pool. To an acquaintance merely it would have been unnoticeable; even to a friend, if it had happened only once or twice, it might have passed undetected; as it was, he could not fail to see that it was there, nor could he fail to puzzle his wits over what the cause of it might be.

During the day he tried to get a word with her in private, but she seemed to anticipate his intention, and contrived that it should be impossible for the request to be made. Once, however, just after the return that afternoon from Boulter's Lock, he had managed to say to her: "There is nothing the matter, is there?" and with complete politeness she had replied: "I have just a touch of a cold. But it is nothing, thanks." And thereupon she had taken up a newspaper, and remarked to Lady

Nottingham that the Eton and Harrow match seemed to have been extraordinarily exciting.

Now, no man, unless he is definitely in love with and enthralled by a woman, will, if he has anything which may be called spirit, stand this sort of thing tamely. Lindfield honestly examined himself to see "if in aught he had offended," could find no cause of offence in himself, and then went through a series of conflicting and unsettling emotions.

He told himself that for some reason she had wished to get on intimate terms with him, and then, her curiosity or whatever it was being satisfied, she had merely opened the hand into which she had taken his and, so to speak, wiped his hand off. This seemed to him a very mean and heartless proceeding, but there it was. She had clearly done this, and if a woman chose to behave like that to a man the only rejoinder consistent with ordinary dignity and self-respect was to take no notice at all, and dismiss her from his mind.

Clearly that was the right thing to do, but instead of doing the right thing he first felt angry, and then sick at heart. Women—those witches—were really rather cruel. They cast a spell over one, and then rode away on their broomsticks, disregarding the poor wretch over whom they had cast it. He was left to go mooning about, until in the merciful course of Nature the spell began to lose its potency and die out. Then, again, he would remember the dignity of man, and repeat to himself his determination to dismiss her and her incomprehensibilities from his mind, and challenge Daisy to some silly game. She, poor wretch, would accept with avidity; but the game, whatever it was, soon seemed to lose its edge and its gaiety. There was something that had clearly gone wrong.

Daisy guessed what that was, and her guess was fairly correct. It seemed to her that for a couple of days Aunt Jeannie had, to put it quite bluntly, run after Lord Lindfield. She had pretty well caught him up, too, for Daisy was fair-minded enough to see that he had not been very agile in getting away from her. He had been quite glad to be caught up, and was evidently charmed by her.

Then, clearly, about the time of her own headache, something had happened; Daisy could see that. Aunt Jeannie, though positively melting with geniality and charming warmth to everybody else, turned on him a shoulder that was absolutely frozen. Why she had done this Daisy could not help guessing, and her solution was that Jeannie had been tremendously attracted by him, and then suddenly seen that somehow it "wouldn't do." Perhaps at this point the sight that Daisy had caught of her aunt and Victor Braithwaite together in the garden supplied a gap in the explanation. Daisy did not like to think that that was it; for, in truth, if it was, there was no doubt whatever that darling Aunt Jeannie had been flirting. But, as Aunt Jeannie had quite ceased to flirt, Daisy was more than willing to forgive her for the miseries of those two dreadful days; she was even willing to forget.

Only Lord Lindfield, it was clear to her, did not quite forget. He was altogether unlike himself. For a little while he would be uproariously cheerful, then his gaiety would go out without a gutter, like a candle suddenly taken out into a gale of wind. And then, perhaps, his eyes would stray about till, for a moment, they fastened on Jeannie, who was probably as entranced by the general joy of life as he had been a minute before. Then he would look puzzled, and then angry, and then puzzled again.

Whatever was passing in Jeannie's mind, she concealed it with supreme success, so that nobody could possibly tell that anything was passing there, or that she had any currents going along below the surface. But she had—currents that were going in the direction she had willed to set them; but for all that they flowed in so strong a tide she hated the flowing of them, and hated herself who had set them moving. She was playing a deep game, and one that had required all her wit to invent, and all her tact to play; but during all this Sunday and the day that followed she observed the effect of her moves, and, though hating them, was well satisfied with their result.

With the tail of her eye, or with half an ear, even while she was in full swing of some preposterous discussion, punctuated with laughter, with Jim Crowfoot, she could observe Lord Lindfield, could see his perplexity and his anger, could hear his attempts to talk and laugh, as if there was nothing to trouble him; could note, before long, the sudden change in his tone, the short monosyllables of answers, the quenched laugh. He was much with Daisy, but Mrs. Halton did not mind that; indeed, it was as she would have had it, for it was clear how little Daisy had the power to hold him, and it was just that which he was beginning now to perceive. She wanted him to understand that very completely, to have it sink down into his nature till it became a part of him.

Yes, her diplomacy was prospering well; already the fruit of it was swelling on the tree. It might be salutary; it was certainly bitter.

CHAPTER XXI.

Jeannie went that night to Lady Nottingham's room to talk to her. She herself was feeling very tired, not with the sound and wholesome tiredness that is the precursor of long sleep and refreshed awakening, but with the restless fatigue of frayed nerves and disquiet mind that leads to intolerable tossings and turnings, and long vigils through the varying greys of dawn and the first chirrupings of birds.

"I have not come for long, dear," she said, "but I had to tell somebody about—about what is happening. It's going so well, too."

Alice saw the trouble in Jeannie's face, and, as a matter of fact, had seen trouble in other faces.

"I haven't had a word with you," she said, "and I don't know what is happening. You seem to have had nothing to say to Lord Lindfield all day. I thought, perhaps, you had given it up. It was too hard for you, dear. I don't wonder you found you could not compass it."

Jeannie gave a little impatient sound; her nerves were sharply on edge.

"Dear Alice," she said, "that is not very clever of you. I thought you would see. However, I am quite glad you don't, for if you don't I am sure Daisy doesn't. I am getting a respite from Daisy's—well, Daisy's loathing of me and my methods. She, like you, probably thinks I have given him back to her."

Jeannie was prowling up and down the room rather in the manner of some restless caged thing. In spite of her tiredness and her disquietude, it seemed to Lady Nottingham that she had never seen her look so beautiful. She looked neither kind nor genial nor sympathetic, but for sheer beauty, though rather formidable, there were no two words to it.

"Sit down, Jeannie," said Alice quietly. "You are only exciting yourself. And tell me about it all. I understand nothing, it seems."

Jeannie paused a moment in her walk, and then fell to pacing the room again.

"No, I'm not exciting myself," she said, "but it is exciting me. I don't stir myself up by walking; I am merely attempting, not very successfully, to walk my excitement off. Oh, Alice, what wild beasts we are at bottom! Prey! Prey! Prey! It is one of the instincts that we—you and I, nice women—are rarely conscious of;

but I doubt whether it is ever quite dormant. Yes, that comes later; I will explain from the beginning.

"The beginning of it all was easy," she said. "It is perfectly easy for any woman to capture the attention of a man like that, even when he is seriously thinking of getting married to a girl. There was no difficulty in making him take me to the concert, in making him neglect Daisy those first two days. He liked me immensely, and, oh! Alice, here was the first extra difficulty, I liked him. We became friends. We mentioned the word friend openly as applied to us. And I felt like—like a man who gets a wild bird to sit on his hand and eat out of it, in order to grab it, and if not to wring its neck, to put it into a cage. I meant to put him into a cage, shut the door, and go away. And then yesterday afternoon in the punt, just after we had made our discovery that we were friends, he confided in me. He told me he was going to settle down and marry! Judge of my rage, my disappointment! I saw that all my efforts up till then had been quite useless. He was still meaning to marry, and, as was right, poor dear, he told the news to his friend. Daisy's name did not come in. Something made us break off—a flash of lightning, I think, and the beginning of the storm. I should have found something to divert the conversation otherwise. It was much better, in view of what I have to do, that I should not officially know to whom he hoped to be married."

Already the calming effect of telling a trouble to a friend was being felt by Jeannie, and she sat down on the sofa near the window, clasping her hands behind her head, and looking not at Alice, but into the dark soft night. A little rain was falling, hissing among the bushes.

"I saw then," she said, "that I had made a stupid mistake. I had thought that by mere friendliness and sympathy and making myself agreeable, and making him admire me (which he did and does), I could get him away from Daisy. I see now how impossible that was. If it is I who am going to take him away, he must feel more than that. He will not leave the girl he intended to marry unless he falls in love in his own manner with some one else. Alice, I believe he is doing so."

Jeannie paused a moment.

"I hate it all," she said, "but I can't help being immensely interested. Now for the part you don't understand, the part that made you think that I had given it all up. It was a bold game, and, I believe, a correct one. I dropped him—d-r-o-p, drop. Why? Simply in order that he might miss me. Of course, I risked failure. He might have shrugged his shoulders, and wondered why I had taken so much trouble to flirt with him, and gone straight away and resumed operations with Daisy. He did go straight back to Daisy, but do you think they are getting on very nicely? I don't. The more he sees of her now, the more he thinks about me. I don't say he has kind thoughts of me; he is puzzled, *but* he doesn't dismiss me. He is angry instead, and hurt. That shows he wants me. He will never propose to Daisy while he feels like that."

There was a short silence. Then Lady Nottingham said,—

"Do you mean you want to make him propose to you?"

"Yes."

The monosyllable came very dryly and unimportantly, as if to a perfectly commonplace inquiry. Then Lady Nottingham, in her turn, got up. Jeannie's restlessness and disquiet seemed to have transferred themselves to her.

"But it is an intolerable rôle," she said. "You cannot play with love like that. It is playing heads and tails with a man's life, or worse. You are playing with his very soul."

"And a month afterwards it will be he who will be playing with another woman's soul," said Jeannie quietly. "You cannot call it love with that sort of man. How many times has he been in love, and what has happened to it all? I am only making myself the chance woman with whom he happens to think himself in love at the time when he proposes to settle down and marry. He shall propose marriage, therefore, to me."

Lady Nottingham's air of comfort had quite left her. Her plump, contented face was puckered into unusual wrinkles.

"No, no, no," she said. "I can't imagine you act like that, Jeannie. It isn't you."

Jeannie's eyes grew suddenly sombre.

"Oh, my dear, it is me," she said, "though I am glad it is a me which is a stranger to you. I hope, as a rule, I don't play pitch-and-toss with other men's souls; but there are circumstances—and those have now arisen—in which I see no other way. At all costs to him I will fulfil my promise to Diana. I will do my best that Daisy shall never know. I do not care what it costs him. And yet that is not quite true. I do care, because I like him. But I cannot measure his possible suffering against Daisy's. It is through him that the need of doing this has come. He has got to suffer for it; and I assure you it isn't he alone who pays, it is I also."

Jeannie rose.

"And I do not yet know if I shall succeed," she said. "He may look with a scornful wonder on my—my somewhat mature charms. He may—though I do not really expect it—still intend to settle down and marry— Daisy. She will accept him, if he does—I have seen enough to know that—and we shall then have to tell her. But I hope that may not happen."

She took up her candle.

"I must go to bed," she said, "for I am dog-tired. But I don't feel so fretted now I have told you. I wish I did not like him. I should not care if I did not. Good-night, dear Alice."

All next day until evening Jeannie continued these tactics. Genial, eager, sympathetic with others, she treated Lord Lindfield, whenever it was necessary to speak to him at all, with the unsmiling civility which a well-bred woman accords to a man she scarcely knows, and does not wish to know better. And all day she saw the growing effect of her policy, for all day he grew more perplexed and more preoccupied with her. She gave him no opportunity of speaking with her alone, for she had planned her day and occupations so that she was all the time in the company of others, and hour by hour his trouble increased. Nor did the trouble spare Daisy. Nothing could be clearer to her eye, with such absolute naturalness did Jeannie manage the situation, than that she now, at any rate, was standing quite aloof from Lord Lindfield.

A few days ago Daisy had told herself that she was glad her aunt liked him, but it should be added that to-day she was equally glad that Jeannie apparently did not. Yet the trouble did not spare Daisy, for if Aunt Jeannie was utterly changed to Lindfield, he seemed to be utterly changed too. He was grave, anxious, preoccupied, and the meaning of it escaped the girl, even as it had escaped Lady Nottingham.

The party had been gradually gathering in the verandah before it was time to dress for dinner that night, and Jeannie, *à propos* of the dressing-bell, had just announced that a quarter of an hour was enough for any nimble woman, with a competent maid.

"She throws things at me, and I catch them and put them on," she said. "If I don't like them I drop them, and the floor of the room looks rather like Carnival-time until she clears up."

But the sense of the meeting was against Jeannie; nobody else could "manage," it appeared, under twenty minutes, and Jim Crowfoot stuck out for half an hour.

"You've got soft things to put on," he said; "but imagine a stiff shirt-cuff hitting you in the eye when your maid threw it. The floor of my room would look not so much like Carnival-time as a shambles."

Lord Lindfield, indeed, alone supported Jeannie.

"I want ten minutes," he said; "neither more nor less. Jim, it's time for you to go, else you will keep us waiting for dinner. I see that Mrs. Halton and I will be left alone at ten minutes past eight, and I at a quarter past."

Jeannie heard this perfectly, but she turned quickly to Lady Nottingham.

"Alice, is it true that you have a post out after dinner?" she said. "Yes? I must go and write a letter, then, before dressing; I particularly want it to get to town to-morrow."

She rose and went in. And at that Lindfield deliberately got up too and followed her. She walked straight through the drawing-room, he a pace or two behind, and out into the hall. And then he spoke to her by name.

She turned round at that. There was no way to avoid giving a reply, and, indeed, she did not wish to, for she believed that the policy of the last two days had ripened.

"Yes, Lord Lindfield?" she said.

"Am I ever going to have a word with you again?" he asked.

Jeannie leant over the banisters; she had already gone up some six stairs.

"But by all means," she said. "I—I too have missed our talks. Things have gone wrong a little? Let us try after dinner to put them straight. We shall find an opportunity."

"Thanks," he said; and it was not only the word that thanked her.

Jeannie's maid must have been a first-rate hand at throwing, if by that simple process she produced in a quarter of an hour that exquisite and finished piece of apparelling which appeared at half-past eight. True, it was Jeannie who wore the jewels and the dress, and her hair it was that rose in those black billows above her shapely head; and the dress, it may be said, was worthy of the wearer. Still, if this was to be arrived at by throwing things, the maid, it was generally felt, must be a competent hurler.

It so happened that everybody was extremely punctual that night, and Jeannie, though quite sufficiently so, the last to appear. Lady Nottingham was even just beginning to allude to the necessary quarter of an hour when she came in.

Lord Lindfield saw her first; he was talking to Daisy. But he turned from her in the middle of a sentence, and said,—

"By Gad!"

It might have been by Gad, but it was by Worth. Four shades of grey, and pearls. Mrs. Beaumont distinctly thought that this was not the sort of dress to dash into the faces of a quiet country party. It was like letting off rockets at a five o'clock tea. Only a woman could dissect the enormity of it; men just stared.

"I know I am not more than one minute late," she said. "Lord Lindfield, Alice has told me to lead you to your doom, which is to take me in.—Alice, they have told us, haven't they?"

CHAPTER XXII.

It seemed to Lord Lindfield that dinner was over that night with unusual swiftness, and that they had scarcely sat down when they rose again for the women to leave the room. Yet, short though it seemed, it had been a momentous hour, for in that hour all the perplexity and the anger that had made his very blood so bitter to him during these last two days had been charmed away from him, and instead, love, like some splendid fever of the spirit, burned there.

Until Jeannie had been friendly, been herself with him again, he had not known, bad as the last two days had been, how deeply and intimately he missed her friendship. That, even that, merely her frank and friendly intercourse, had become wine to him; he thirsted and longed for it, and even it, now that it was restored to him, mounted to his head with a sort of psychic intoxication. Yet that was but the gift she had for the whole world of her friends; what if there was something for him behind all that, which should be his alone, and not the world's—something to which this wine was but as water?

At dinner this had been but the side she showed to all the world, but there was better coming. She had promised him a talk that night, and by that he knew well she did not mean just the intercourse of dinner-talk, which all the table might share in, but a talk like those they had had before by the roadside when the motor broke down, or in the punt while the thunderstorm mounted in hard-edged, coppery clouds up the sky. The last thing they had spoken of then was friendship, and he had told her, he remembered, how he hoped to settle down and marry. He hoped that she would of her own accord speak of friendship again; that would be a thing of good omen, for again, as before, he would speak of his hope of settling down and marrying. Only he would speak of it differently now.

For him the hour had struck; there was no choice of deliberation possible any more to him. He did not look on the picture of quiet domesticity any more, and find it pleasing; he did not look on himself, count up his years, and settle, with a content that had just one grain of resignation in it, that it was time for him to make what is called a home. He looked at Jeannie, and from the ocean of love a billow came, bore him off his feet, and took him seawards. She, the beauty of her face, the soft curves of her neck, the grace and suppleness of her body, were no longer, as had been the case till now, the whole of the woman whom he loved. Now they were but the material part of her; he believed and knew that he loved something that was more essentially Jeannie than these—he loved her soul and spirit.

Late this love had come to him, for all his life he had stifled its possibility of growth by being content with what was more material; but at last it had dawned on him, and he stood now on the threshold of a world that was as new as it was bewildering. Yet, for all its bewilderment, he saw at a glance how real it was, and how true. It was the light of the sun that shone there which made those shadows which till now he had thought to be in themselves so radiant.

It was about half-past ten when Jeannie and Lord Lindfield cut out of a bridge-table simultaneously. They had been playing in the billiard-room, and strolled out together, talking. In the hall outside, that pleasant place of books and shadows and corners, Jeannie paused and held out her hand to him.

"Lord Lindfield," she said, "I have been a most utter beast to you these last two days, and I am sorry—I am indeed. You have got a perfect right to ask for explanations, and—and there aren't any. That is the best explanation of all; you can't get behind it. Will you, then, be generous and shake hands, and let us go on where we left off?"

He took her hand.

"That is exactly the condition I should have made," he said.

"What?"

"That we should go on where we left off. Do you remember what you were talking about?"

She had sat down in a low chair by the empty fireplace, and he drew another close up to hers, and at right angles to it. Just above was a pair of shaded candles, so that he, sitting a little further off, was in shadow, whereas the soft light fell full on to her. Had she seen his face more clearly, she might have known that her task was already over, that Daisy had become but a shadow to him, and that he was eager and burning to put the coping-stone on to what she had accomplished. But she remembered the scene in the punt; she remembered that immediately after she had spoken of friendship, he, like a friend, had confided to her his intention of settling down and marrying. This time, therefore, she would speak in a more unmistakable way.

"Yes, yes, I remember indeed," she said; "and it was the last good hour I have had between that and this. But

I am not blaming you, Lord Lindfield, except, perhaps, just a little bit."

He leant forward, and his voice trembled.

"Why do you blame me," he asked, "even a little bit?"

Jeannie laughed.

"No, I don't think I can tell you," she said. "I should get scarlet. Yet, I don't know; I think it would make you laugh, too, and it is always a good thing to laugh. So turn away, and don't look at me when I am scarlet, since it is unbecoming. Well, I blame you a little bit, because you were a little bit tactless. A charming woman—one, anyhow, who was trying to be charming—had just been talking to you about friendship, and you sighed a smile in a yawn, as it were—do you know Browning?—he is a dear—and said: 'I am going to settle down and marry.' Now, not a word. I am going to scold you. Had we been two girls talking together, and had just made vows of friendship, it would have been utterly tactless for the one to choose that exact moment for saying she was going to be married; and I am sure no two boys in similar conditions would ever have done such a thing."

Again Jeannie laughed.

"It sounds so funny now," she said. "But it was such a snub. I suppose you thought we were getting on too nicely. Oh, how funny! I have never had such a thing happen to me before. So I blame you just a little bit. I was rather depressed already. A thunderstorm was coming, and it was going to be Sunday, and so I wanted everybody to be particularly nice to me."

He gave a little odd awkward sort of laugh, and jerked himself a little more forward in his chair.

"Mayn't I look?" he said. "I don't believe you are scarlet. Besides, I have to say I am sorry. I can't say I am sorry to the carpet."

Jeannie paused for a moment before she replied; something in his voice, though still she could not see his face clearly, startled her. It sounded changed, somehow, full of something suppressed, something serious. But she could not risk a second fiasco; she had to play her high cards out, and hope for their triumph.

"You needn't say it," she said. "And so let us pass to what I suggested, and what you would have made, you told me, a condition of your forgiving me. Friendship! What a beautiful word in itself, and what a big one! And how little most people mean by it. A man says he is a woman's friend because he lunches with her once a month; a woman says she is a man's friend because they have taken a drive round Hyde Park in the middle of the afternoon!"

Jeannie sat more upright in her chair, leaning forward towards him. Then she saw him more clearly, and the hunger of his face, the bright shining of his eyes, endorsed what she had heard in his voice. Yet she was not certain—not quite certain.

"Oh, I don't believe we most of us understand friendship at all," she said. "It is not characteristic of our race to let ourselves feel. Most English people neither hate nor love, nor make friends in earnest. I think one has to go South—South and East—to find hate and love and friends, just as one has to go South to find the sun. Do you know the Persian poet and what he says of his friend:

'A book of verses underneath the bough, A loaf of bread, a jug of wine, and thou Beside me singing in the wilderness, The wilderness were paradise enow.'

Ah, that is more my notion of friendship, of the ideal of friendship, the thing that makes Paradise of the desert."

He got up quickly and stood before her, speaking hoarsely and quickly.

"It does not matter what you call it," he said. "I know what you mean. I call it love, that is all—Jeannie, Jeannie——"

He seized both her hands in his roughly, brutally almost, and covered them with kisses.

"Ah, it is done!" said Jeannie quickly, and half to herself. Then she rose too, and wrenched her hands from him.

"Have you gone mad?" she said. "Stand out of my way, please."

But she had not reckoned on the strength of the passion she had raised. For one moment he looked at her in blank astonishment, but he did not move. She could not get by him without violence. Then he advanced a step again towards her, as if he would have caught her to him. Jeannie put both her arms in front of her; she had turned pale to the lips.

"Not till you have told me——"

"I have nothing to tell you, except that I thought you were a gentleman and a friend. There is some one coming out of the billiard-room."

Daisy appeared in the doorway at the moment.

"The rubber's over already," she said, "just two hands. Won't you and Lord Lindfield———"

She stopped suddenly. It was clear he had not heard her, for, with arms still held out, he faced Jeannie, unconscious of any one but her.

"Jeannie———" he began again.

Jeannie did not look at him.

"Please let me pass," she said.—"No, Daisy, I think I have played enough. I am going upstairs. It is late. I am tired."

CHAPTER XXIII.

Jeannie went straight to her room. It was done, even as she had said, and her heart bled for her triumph. Yet she did not for a moment repent it. Had it been necessary to do it again, she would again have gone through the same hateful scene, and her scorn of herself weighed light even now with the keeping of the promise she had made by the bedside of Diana. But the thing had been worse than she had anticipated; it was no superficial desire she had aroused in him, but the authentic fire. But that made Daisy the safer: a man was not often in earnest like that.

But still the future was unplanned for; she had made her scene, scored her point, and the curtain, dramatically speaking, should have descended. But in real life the curtain did not descend; life insisted that there were no such things as curtains; it made one go on. She knew, too, that Lindfield would not take this as final; she had to think of something which should make it final. In any case she could not contemplate stopping in the house, with him there, and decided to go back to town to-morrow, cutting her stay here short by a day. She would go early, before any one was down; Alice would invent and explain for her.

A note, hastily scribbled, settled this. "It is done, Alice," she wrote, "and I feel satisfied and utterly miserable. Daisy does not exist for him. I shall go back to town early to-morrow, dear. Will you make some excuse? I know you will understand."

But the more important matter was not settled so easily. She had to show poor Lindfield unmistakably that her rejection of him was quite irrevocable. What interpretation he put on her conduct mattered but little, as long as he clearly understood that. And then a means occurred to her which was quite simple and quite sufficient. She wrote a couple of lines to Victor.

"My dearest," she said, "I must go to town early to-morrow, and shall not see you till you come up the day after. And I want you to announce our engagement at once. I should like it to be in the evening papers to-morrow. Tell them yourself down here. I write this in great haste. All love."

Jeannie rang for her maid to get these delivered, dismissed her for the night, and sat down to think over what she had done. She was still tremulous from it. To a man she really liked, and to a girl whom she tenderly loved, she had made herself vile, but it was still her sincere hope that neither would ever know the reason for what she had done. They must write her down a flirt; they had every reason for doing so.

She rose and looked at herself a moment in the long mirror beside the dressing-table. "You beast!" she said to herself. But there was another thought as well. "Diana, my dear," she said, as if comforting her.

It had been settled that Jeannie was to live with Lady Nottingham till the end of the season, and the latter had given her two charming rooms in the Grosvenor Square house, so that she could make things home-like about her for the few weeks before she would go down to her own house in the country. Little household gods had arrived and been unpacked while she was in the country, and she occupied herself during this solitary day in London with the arrangement of them. There were not many, for she did not tend to buy, but there were a few "bits of things" which she had got in Rome, a Cinquecento bas-relief, a couple of Florentine copies of the Della Robbia heads, and some few pieces of Italian needlework. All these took some little time to dispose satisfactorily in the room, and that done, she proceeded to the arrangement of her writing-table. She liked to have photographs there: there was one of Daisy and

Diana, two mites of ten years old and four years old, lovingly entwined, Daisy's head resting on her sister's shoulder; there was one of Victor as he was now, and another as he had been when an Eton boy; there were half a dozen others, and among them one of Diana, signed and dated, which Diana had given her hardly more than a year ago in Paris.

All this arranging took up the greater part of the day, and she kept herself to her work, forcing her mind away from those things which really occupied it, and making it attend to the manual business of putting books in shelves and pictures on the walls; but about tea-time there was nothing more to occupy her here, and by degrees her thoughts drifted back to Bray and her friends—or were they enemies?—there. It was no use thinking of it or them, for there was nothing more to be contrived or planned or acted, no problem for her to dig at, no crisis to avert.

She had finished everything, and there was nothing left for her to do except be silent, and hope perhaps by degrees to win Daisy back again. How Daisy reconstructed things in her own mind Jeannie did not know, and, indeed, the details of such reconstruction she did not particularly want to know. She had taken Lord Lindfield away from the girl, for a mere caprice, apparently, for the love of annexation characteristic of flirts, while all the time she was engaged to Victor Braithwaite. And having made mischief like this, she had run away. It was like a child who, having from sheer wantonness set fire to something, runs to a safe distance and watches it burn.

Jeannie had ordered the carriage to come round at six to take her for a drive, and a few minutes before, though it was barely six yet, she had heard something drive up and stop at the door, and supposed that before long her maid would tell her that it was round. Even as she thought this she heard steps come along the passage outside, then her door opened.

Daisy entered. She was very pale, but in each cheek there flamed one high spot of colour. She stood quite still by the door for a moment, looking at her aunt, then closed it and advanced into the room.

"It is true, then, Aunt Jeannie," she said, "that you are engaged to Victor Braithwaite? I came up from Bray to ask you that, to know it from your own lips."

Jeannie did not move, nor did she give Daisy any word of conventional greeting.

"It is quite true," she said.

Daisy began pulling off her gloves.

"I congratulate you," she said. "It came as rather a surprise to me. Aunt Alice told me. I think she understood why it was a surprise to me. I wonder if you do?"

Daisy appeared to be keeping a very firm hand on herself. There was no question that she was speaking under some tremendous stress of emotion, but her voice was quite quiet. It trembled a little, but that was all, and it seemed to Jeannie that that tremor was of anger more than of self-pity or sorrow. She was glad—in so far as she was glad of anything—that this was so.

"I see you don't answer me," said Daisy, "and, indeed, there is no need. But I want an answer to this question, Aunt Jeannie. Why did you do it? Don't you think I have a right to know that?"

For one moment it occurred to Jeannie to profess and to persist in professing that she did not know what Daisy meant. But that would have been useless, and worse than useless—unworthy. In her utter perplexity she tried another tack.

"Is it my fault that he fell in love with me?" she said.

"Did you not mean him to?" asked Daisy. "And all the time, while you meant him to, you were engaged to Mr. Braithwaite."

There was still anger in Daisy's voice. Jeannie felt she could bear that; what she felt she could not bear would be if Daisy broke down. So she encouraged that.

"I do not see by what right you question me," she said. "Lord Lindfield fell in love with me; last night he proposed to me. Ask him why he did that."

"He did that because you fascinated and dazzled him," said Daisy; "because you meant him to fall in love with you."

"Then I wonder you have not more spirit," said Jeannie. "You see how easily he turned from you to me. Can you then believe he was ever in love with you? You may have wanted to marry him; at least——"

And then she paused, knowing she had made the most ghastly mistake, and not knowing how to remedy it. Daisy saw her mistake.

"Then you did know that it was possible he would ask me to marry him," she said. "I wondered if you knew that. It makes it complete now I know that you did. So it comes to this, that you cut me out just in order to flirt with him. Thank you, Aunt Jeannie, thank you."

And then there came into Daisy's voice what Jeannie dreaded to hear; the hard tone of anger died out of it, it became gentle, and it became miserable. She sat down at Jeannie's writing-table, covering her face with her hands.

"Oh, I beseech you," she said, "cannot you undo the spell that you cast so easily? Oh, Aunt Jeannie, do, do; and I will forget all that has happened, and—and love you again. I want to do that. But I loved him; it was only quite lately I knew that, but it is so. Have you not enough? Isn't it enough that you will marry the man you love? I did not think you could be so cruel. Do you hate me, or what is it?"

Jeannie made a little hopeless gesture with her hands.

"Oh, Daisy, I didn't know that you loved him," she said. "Indeed, I did not. But, my dear, he did not love you. How could he have if he behaved as he has behaved?"

"You made him," said Daisy. "You——" Then once again anger flamed into her voice. "Ah, what a true friend you have been to me!" she said. "Were you as true a friend to Diana too?"

She had taken up one of the photographs, that which represented her and Diana together.

"Here we are together," she said, "and we thank you. Here is Diana by herself———"

And then she stopped abruptly. Her eye had fallen on the photograph of Diana which she had given only last year to Jeannie. It was signed "Diana, 1907." She drew it out of its frame.

"Aunt Jeannie," she said, quickly, "in what year did Diana die?"

Jeannie turned to her suddenly at this most unexpected question, and saw what it was that Daisy held in her hand. She made a desperate effort to turn Daisy's attention away at any cost.

"Daisy, we were talking about Lord Lindfield," she said. "What reason had he ever given you to make you think he loved you? And has he not given you a strong reason for showing he did not?"

Daisy looked at her for a moment, and then back to the photograph.

"She died five years ago," she said. "But this is signed 1907, last year."

Once again Jeannie tried to turn Daisy's attention.

"And if he did fall in love with me, what then?" she said. "You assume it is all my fault."

Daisy looked at her steadily a moment, and then back at the photograph.

"Yes, yes," she said. "But you were with Diana when she died, were you not? When did she die?"

Jeannie covered her face with her hands a moment, thinking intently, and then Daisy spoke again.

"Why was I told she died five years ago?" she asked. "You told me so yourself. Were you hiding anything?"

Again Daisy paused.

"Her husband came to England after her death," she said. "He stopped with you, I remember, when I was living with you."

Once again she paused.

"Was there something dreadful, something disgraceful?" she asked. "Aunt Jeannie, I must know. I must!"

CHAPTER XXIV.

Jeannie got up out of her chair, where she had been sitting ever since Daisy entered. Daisy as she spoke had risen also from the writing-table, and, still holding the photograph of Diana in her hand, stood by her.

"You must give me a moment, Daisy," she said. "I have got to think. And, my dear, while I am thinking do not try to guess. I can't bear that you should guess. I would sooner tell you than that."

Daisy was very white, and the bright spot of anger that burnt in her cheeks when she entered the room had smouldered away. She nodded without spoken reply.

Jeannie moved away from Daisy, and sat down in the window-seat at the far end of the room. Already Daisy had guessed that there was something disgraceful. Daisy remembered, too, that after Diana's supposed death her husband had come to England. And then for one moment Jeannie's spirit rose in impotent revolt against the bitter cruelty of this chance by which Daisy had seen Diana's photograph. She herself, perhaps, had been careless and culpable, in putting it on her table; but she had been so preoccupied with all the perplexities of this last week that the danger had not ever so faintly occurred to her. But now by this fatal oversight Daisy had already guessed perilously near the truth.

She herself could invent no story to account for these things, and if Daisy was told the whole truth, of which she guessed so much, that other bitterness, the sense that Jeannie had cruelly betrayed her, would be removed. She could comfort Daisy again, and (this was sweet to herself also) show her how she loved her. She had done her very best to keep her promise to Diana, and she had not spared herself in doing so; and now, in spite of her efforts, so hard to make and so ungrudgingly made, half the truth was known to Daisy. It seemed to her that the other half would heal rather than hurt.

She went back, and, standing in front of the girl, held out her hands to her. But Daisy made no response to the gesture, and, indeed, moved a little away. That, again, cut Jeannie like a lash, but she knew the pain of it would be only temporary. In a few minutes now Daisy would understand.

"I am going to tell you," she said, "and as I tell you, my dear, I want you to keep on thinking to yourself that Diana was your sister, your only sister, and—and that you used to play together and love each other when you were children. And, dear Daisy, you must try to be—not to be a girl only when I tell you this. You are a girl, but you are a woman also, and you must bear this like a woman who is hearing about her sister."

Once again Jeannie longed to take Daisy in her arms and tell her, holding that dear head close to her bosom. But it was not time for that yet.

"You were told five years ago," she said, "that your sister was dead. She was not, Daisy; she died last year only, soon after I went abroad. And she died in my arms, dear, thank Heaven, because I loved her. And she loved me, Daisy. Oh, darling, you must bear this. I tried to spare you the knowledge, for I promised Diana that, but by ill-chance you have guessed so much that I think it better to tell you all. And you mustn't judge Diana, poor dear, or condemn her. The time has quite gone by for that, and, besides, she was your sister, and at the end the thing she wanted most in all the world was that you should not know. Remember that. Women have a hard time in this world, Daisy. Some are married unhappily, and though Diana's husband loved her very truly and tenderly it was not a happy marriage. At the time when you were told she was dead she was not, but she had left her husband. For the love he bore her he did not divorce her. Yes, dear, it was that."

Again Jeannie paused. As the moment came near it was all she could do to get the words out. Yet when Daisy knew all, out of the hurt would come some healing. Jeannie could make her feel how she loved her.

"She lived in Paris after she left her husband," she continued. "She lived for a time with the man for whom she deserted him. She wanted love—women do—you and I do. She—she got love. After a while there was another man. Yes, my dear, it was he. We needn't name him any more than we did just now when we spoke of him."

Daisy sat quite still for a moment; for all that her face expressed she might never have heard. Then a sudden little tremor shook her, and she tore the photograph of Diana which she held across and across, and threw the fragments on the floor.

"Ah, Daisy, you are cruel," said Jeannie.

Daisy did not reply, and then suddenly her mouth began to tremble, and tears ready to fall gathered in her eyes. It had hurt her cruelly, and it was but the instinctive rebellion of one in sudden and incontrollable pain that had made her tear the photograph. But, as Jeannie had foreseen, with the hurt came healing.

It was not necessary to say any more, for she saw that already Daisy was beginning to understand all that she had thought so incomprehensible, and so vile when it was comprehended, in her, and the comprehension brought with it the knowledge of the love and tenderness from which these things sprang. And this time it was Daisy who held out her hands to Jeannie, but falteringly, as if doubtful whether she dared. But she need not have been afraid; next moment she was clasped close, and with the sense of love surrounding and encompassing her the tears came, and she sobbed her heart out. And even when the tumult of her weeping had abated, it was but disjointedly that the words came.

"And so it was because of that, Aunt Jeannie," she whispered, "because you had promised Diana that you would do your best to keep it from me?"

"Yes, my darling, but I have failed," said Jeannie.

"But how splendidly," whispered Daisy. "I should like to have f-failed like that. And you were content that I should think you a b-beast, and that he should?"

"No, dear, not content quite. But it was the best I could think of."

"And Mr. Braithwaite?" said Daisy. "Could you be content that he should think so?"

Jeannie paused a moment before she replied. What she must say, if she answered this, would hurt Daisy again, but again there was healing there.

"I knew he would never think me a beast," she said at length. "I knew he trusted me absolutely."

"And I didn't," said Daisy.

"No, dear, you didn't. But never mind that."

"I can't help minding that. I thought—I thought everything disgusting about you. Oh, Aunt Jeannie, but I did try so much not to! I did try to behave well, to realize that you and he had fallen in love with each other, and that it was neither your fault nor his. But when Aunt Alice told me that you were engaged to Mr. Braithwaite, then I broke down. And when you told me you had known that I hoped to marry Lord Lindfield, then it was complete to my mind. I thought—oh! I have spoilt it all. It can never be the same again. And I did so long for you to come home a week ago. I did love you."

Jeannie stroked Daisy's hair gently for a moment or two.

"You speak of spoiling love," she said. "That is not easy to do. In fact, it can't be done. So don't have any fears on that point, my darling."

Daisy was silent for a while.

"And if he asks you why you did it?" she said.

Jeannie considered this.

"I may have to tell him," she said. "It all depends. Probably you don't understand that."

"No; tell me," said Daisy.

"If he appeals to me in the name of his love for me, I think I shall have to tell him," said Jeannie. "I don't want to; I shall do my best not to. But there is a claim, that of love, which is dominant. I did not mean him to fall in love with me, dear; I meant him only to be detached from you. But bigger issues, I am afraid, have come in. You must trust me to do the best I can. I think you will trust me, will you not?"

Daisy clung closer for a moment, and then she sat up.

"Yes. And I haven't even said I am sorry, and I am sure I need not. Aunt Jeannie, I think I want to go away alone for a little. I want, yes, I want to cry a little more, but by myself. Do you understand?"

"Yes, my dear. But will you not stop here to-night? You could telegraph to Alice, and you might add that we were friends. She would like to know that."

Daisy mopped her eyes.

"I like to know it," she said.

She got up. Just in front of her were the fragments of the torn photograph. She saw them and half shuddered at them. And Jeannie, all tenderness, knew that things were not right with Daisy yet. There was still another wound which must be healed.

"Oh, Daisy!" she said. "You must never let yourself be black and bitter like that. You tore the photograph up; it lies there still."

"Oh, I can't touch it," said Daisy.

Jeannie looked at her quietly, patiently.

"Your sister," she said. "Diana. Have you forgotten what she made me promise? She was so sorry, too; I think she would have given all the world if what she had done could be undone. Not a day passed without her being sorry. Daisy!"

Daisy stood quite still for a moment, then she suddenly knelt down on the floor and picked the fragments up, kissing them as she did so.

"Oh, poor Di," she said—"poor, poor Di!"

CHAPTER XXV.

The carriage had waited long before this, but when Daisy left her Jeannie went out for a breath of evening air. London, to her eyes, was looking very hot and tired, a purplish heat-haze hung in the sky, and the grass of the Park was yellow with the scorching of the last week, and grey with dust.

Yet somehow it all brought a sense of extraordinary peace and refreshment to Jeannie. She, too, felt mentally hot and tired, but she knew that whatever scene it might be necessary to go through with Tom Lindfield, the worst was over. For, all unwittingly indeed, his had been the fault, and though Jeannie liked him and hated the idea both of his suffering and his possible bitterness and anger against her, all that was in the nature of justice; acts have always their consequences, and those who have committed them must bear what follows. But poor Daisy had done nothing; it was for the fault of others that her soul had been in the grip of resentment, jealousy, and anger, which had embittered and poisoned her days and nights.

But that, all at any rate that was bitter in it, had now passed. She saw the meaning of her suffering; it was no longer a blind and wicked force. And though one love had to be left to wither and die in her heart, Jeannie knew well that the love between Daisy and her, which all this week had been blighted, was full of fresh-springing shoots again, which would help to cover over the bare place.

Then, for herself, more precious than all was that sense of that great love which, she believed, had never suffered the dimness of a moment's doubt. Victor had seen her acting in a way that was impossible for him to understand, but he had quite refused, so Jeannie believed, to let his mind even ask a why or wherefore, still less conjecture any answer. His own love for her and the absolute certainty of her love for him were things so huge that nothing else could be compared with them. They stood like great mountains, based on the earth but reaching into the heavens, firm and imperishable, and if anything could come between his vision and them, it could be no more than a mist-wreath which would presently pass, and could no more shake or invalidate their stability than the grasses and flowers that waved in the pleasant meadow beneath them.

And had Jeannie but known it she would have found more comfort yet in the thought of Daisy, for at this moment Daisy, alone in her room, though weeping a little now and then, was thinking not of herself at all, not even of Lindfield, but of Jeannie. Daisy was generous and warm-hearted to the core, and passionate had been her self-reproach at her complete misunderstanding of her aunt, at her utter failure even to ask herself whether there was not something about it all that she did not understand.

How nobly different Victor Braithwaite had been, who, so it seemed, had assumed there must be some undercurrent of which he knew nothing, and was quite content to leave it at that. Jeannie had said she loved him; he wanted nothing more. But Daisy knew also that Jeannie loved her; what she did not know then, but was beginning to know now, was what love meant; how it can bear even to be completely misunderstood by those it loves, if only, in spite of their ignorance and misjudgment, it can help them. To Daisy, hitherto, love had been something assertive; to-day she was learning that it is based on a self-surrender made with the same passionateness as are its conquests.

The rest of the party were coming up next day, and it did not surprise Jeannie to find a telegram waiting for her when she came in from Tom Lindfield. He asked if he might call and see her next morning, saying that he would come at twelve unless she put him off.

It needed but a moment's reflection to make her decide that in bare justice she could not refuse. She shrank from it; she dreaded the thought of seeing him again, of listening to his just and passionate reproaches; she dreaded also the possibility that she might once again have to give up Diana's secret. But, since he wished it, she must see him.

Next morning she told Daisy she expected him, so that there should be no possibility of their meeting by chance on the stairs or in Jeannie's room, and sat waiting for him alone. She could not prepare herself in any way for the interview, since she could not tell in the least what form it would take. She tried not to be afraid, but—but she had treated him abominably. So, at least, he must think, and with perfect justice.

He was announced, and came in. As with Daisy yesterday, they did not greet one another. She was sitting at her writing-table, but did not rise, and for a moment he stood opposite her, just looking at her with those blue, boyish eyes which she knew could be so merry, but did not know could be so dumbly, hopelessly sad.

Then he spoke, quite quietly.

"You ran away unexpectedly, Mrs. Halton," he said.

"Yes; I thought it was best."

"Miss Daisy also left yesterday. I suppose you have seen her?" he said.

"Yes, she spent the night here."

"Are you friends?"

"Yes."

Tom Lindfield sat down on the arm of the low chair opposite the writing-table.

"That's the cleverest thing I've ever heard," he said. "I think you owe me something, and I think you ought to tell me how you managed it. If she has forgiven you, perhaps I might."

"No. I can't tell you how I managed it," said Jeannie.

"You quite refuse?"

"Quite."

He paused a moment.

"I suppose she asked you a certain question," he said, "which I also want to ask you. Is it true you are engaged to that nice fellow—Braithwaite, I mean?"

"Quite true."

Still quite quietly he got up, took out a cigarette, and looked about for matches. He found some on the chimney-piece, lit his cigarette, and came back to her.

"I beg your pardon," he said. "I didn't ask if I might smoke here? Thanks. Mrs. Halton, I don't know if you have ever fallen in love. I have, once."

His voice rose a little over this, as if with suppressed anger. Jeannie longed almost that he should get angry. This quietness was intolerable. And she tried to sting him into anger.

"I should have thought you had fallen in love more than once," she said.

This was no good.

"You would have been wrong, then," he said. "I should have thought so too till just lately. But I have just found out that I never loved before. I—I did everything else, but I did not love."

"You loved Daisy, do you mean?" she asked.

He flamed up for a moment.

"Ah, there is no good in saying that," he said, sharply. "What can be the use of it? I met the woman—there is only one—and she led me to believe that she cared for me. And when I told her that I loved her she said she had thought I was a gentleman and a friend."

Jeannie felt her heart melt within her.

"Yes, yes, I am sorry," she said.

"That is no good, I am afraid," said he. "You have got to tell me why you did it. We are man and woman, you and I. I cannot believe you did it out of sheer wantonness, from the desire to make me miserable, and, I am afraid, to some extent, to make Miss Daisy miserable. I don't see what you were to gain by it. Also you risked something since you were engaged all the time to Braithwaite. And the only thing I can think of is that for some reason you wished to get between Miss Daisy and myself. I suppose you thought I had been a bad lot—I daresay I had—and did not want me to marry her. But wasn't that an infernally cruel way of doing it?"

Jeannie said nothing, but after a long silence she looked at him.

"Have you finished?" she asked. "I have nothing to say to you, no explanation to give."

Once again, and more violently, his anger, his resentment at the cruelty of it, boiled over.

"No, I have not finished," he said. "I am here to tell you that you have done an infernally cruel thing, for I take it that it was to separate Miss Daisy and me that you did it. You have been completely successful, but—but for me it has been rather expensive. I gave you my heart, I tell you. And you stamped on it. I can't mend it."

Then that died out and his voice trembled.

"It's broken," he said—"just broken."

Jeannie put out her hands towards him in supplication.

"I am sorry," she said.

"I tell you that is no good," he said, and on the words his voice broke again. "Oh, Jeannie, is it final? Is it really true? For Heaven's sake tell me that you have been playing this jest, trick—what you like—on me, to test me, to see if I really loved you. You made me love you— you taught me what love meant. I have seen and judged the manner of my past life, and—and I laid it all down, and I laid myself down at your feet, so that you and love should re-make me."

Jeannie leant forward over the table, hiding her face in her hands.

"Oh, stop—for pity's sake stop," she said. "I have had a good deal to bear. I never guessed you would love me like that; I only meant you, at first, to be attracted by me, as you have been by other women. It is true that I was determined that you should not marry Daisy, and I knew that if you really got to love her nothing would stand in your way. I had to make it impossible for you to fall in love with her. It was to save you and her."

Jeannie felt she was losing her head; the sight of this man in his anger and his misery confused and bewildered her. She got up suddenly.

"I don't know what I am saying," she said.

"You said it was to save her and me," he said, quietly. "To save us from what?"

She shook her head.

"I don't know," she said. "I was talking nonsense."

"I am very sure you were not. And it is only just that I should know. By my love for you—for I can think of nothing more sacred to me than that—I bid you tell me. It is my right. Considering what you have done to me, it is no more than my right."

It had happened as Jeannie feared it might. She felt her throat go suddenly dry, and once she tried to speak without being able. Then she commanded her voice again.

"You were in Paris two years ago," she said. "There was a woman there who lived in the Rue Chalgrin. She called herself Madame Rougierre."

"Well?" said he.

"Daisy's sister," said Jeannie, with a sob.

She turned away from him as she spoke, and leant against the bookcase behind her table. It was a long time before he moved, and then, still with back turned, she heard him approach her, and he took her hand and kissed it.

"I love and I honour you," he said.

Jeannie gave one immense sigh.

"Oh, Tom," she said, "you are a man!"

"It is of your making, then," said he.

CHAPTER XXVI.

Easter fell late next year, but spring had come early, and had behaved with unusual sweetness and constancy, for from the middle of March to mid-April there had been a series of days from which winter had definitely departed. In most years April produces two or three west-wind days of enervating and languorous heat, but then recollects itself and peppers the confiding Englishman with hail and snow, blown as out of a pea-shooter from the northeast, just to remind him that if he thinks that summer is going to begin just yet he is woefully mistaken. But this year the succession of warm days had been so uninterrupted that Lady Nottingham had made the prodigious experiment of asking a few people down to Bray for a week-end party at Easter itself.

She was conscious of her amazing temerity, for she knew well that anything might happen; that the river, instead of being at the bottom of the garden, might so change its mind about their relative positions that in a few hours the garden would be at the bottom of the river, or, again, this bungalow of a house might be riddled and pierced with arctic blasts.

But, in spite of these depressing possibilities, she particularly wanted to have a few, a very few, people down for that Sunday. They had all a special connection with Bray. Things had happened there before, and it was a party of healed memories that was to gather there. If, after all, the weather turned out to be hopelessly unpropitious, they could all sit in a ring round the fire, holding each other's hands. She felt sure they would like to do that. Probably there would be a great many *tête-à-têtes* in various corners, or, if it were warm, in various punts. But she felt sure that they would all hold hands in the intervals of these.

Jeannie and Victor had been married in the autumn, and since then they had practically disappeared, surrounded by a glow of their own happiness. They had sunk below the horizon, but from the horizon there had, so to speak, come up a brilliant illumination like an aurora borealis.

But Lady Nottingham considered that they had aurora-ed quite long enough. They had no right to keep all their happiness to themselves; it was their duty to diffuse it, and let other people warm their hands and hearts at it. She had written what is diplomatically known as a "strong note" to say so, and she had mentioned that she was not alone in considering that they were being rather selfish. Tom Lindfield thought so too. He openly averred that he was still head-over-ears in love with Jeannie, and he wished to gratify his passion by seeing her again, and having copious opportunities given him of solitary talks with her. He did not object (this was all part of the message that Lady Nottingham sent Jeannie from him) to Victor's coming with her, but he would be obliged if Victor would kindly make up his mind to efface himself a good deal. Otherwise he had better stop away.

Tom proposed to come down to Bray for Easter, and would be much obliged if Jeannie would come too. He did not ask her to set aside any other engagements she might have, because he was perfectly well aware that she had no other engagement than that tiresome and apparently permanent one of burying herself in the country with Victor.

Jeannie received this letter at breakfast down at their house in Hampshire. She read it aloud to her husband.

"What a darling he is," she said. "Victor, I shall go. I love that man."

"I know you do. He isn't a bad sort. Do you want me to come too?"

"Oh, I shan't go unless you do," said Jeannie, quickly.

"Right. It's a confounded nuisance, though, but I suppose you must. How many days do you want to stop there?"

"Oh, till Tuesday or Wednesday, I suppose. Perhaps Tom would come back with us here after that."

Victor got up and moved round the table, till he stood by his wife's chair.

"No, I don't think he will," he said. "Fact is, Jeannie, I asked him to come here a week or two ago, and he wrote me an awfully nice letter back, but said he thought he wouldn't. I didn't tell you before, for there was no use in it. But after that I don't think I should ask him if I were you."

Jeannie was silent a moment.

"But he wants to see me now," she said.

"I know. But I don't think he wants to be with us alone. You understand that, I expect."

Jeannie sighed.

"Poor Tom!" she said. "Yet I don't know why I say 'poor.' I think he likes life."

"I don't think he loves it as you and I do."

Jeannie's eyes suddenly filled with tears.

"I am awfully sorry for that," she said. "Sometimes I feel frightfully guilty, and then suddenly on the top of that I feel innocent. Oh, to be plain, I feel more than innocent. I feel dreadfully laudable. And then, to do me justice, I put up a little prayer that I may not become a prig or a donkey."

He laughed.

"Please, don't," he said. "I should not know you. But you made a man of him."

"Ah, yes; he has told you that. It is not the case. He made a man of himself."

Victor held up his hand.

"I don't want to know what happened," he said. "I am quite content to leave it. He became a man, and you were always my beloved."

Some backward surge of memory stirred in Jeannie.

"Quite always?" she said. "You never wanted to ask me about it?"

"No, dear, never," he said. "Not because I was complacent or anything of that kind, but simply because we loved each other."

This, then, was the foundation of Lady Nottingham's Easter party. Jeannie and her husband would come, and so, as a corollary, Lord Lindfield would come. Then there would be the newly-engaged couple, namely, Daisy and Willie Carton. Either of them would go, as steel filings go to the magnet, wherever the other was, and without the least sense of compunction Lady Nottingham told each of them separately that the other was coming to her. She had been rather late in doing this, and, as a matter of fact, Willie, no longer hoping for it, had made another engagement. But he did not even frown or consider that. He wrote a cheerful, scarcely apologetic note to Mrs. Beaumont, merely saying he found he could not come. Nature and art alike—and Mrs. Beaumont was a subtle compound of the two— allow much latitude to lovers, and she did not scold him.

At this stage in her proceedings Lady Nottingham suddenly abandoned the idea of a party at all. There was Victor and Jeannie, and their corollary, Tom Lindfield; there was Daisy and her corollary, Willie; there was herself. Gladys would be there too, and—and it was necessary to provide light conversation in case everybody was too much taken up with everybody else, and Jim Crowfoot would, no doubt, supply it. A very short telephonic pause was succeeded by the assurance that he would.

CHAPTER XXVII.

Two days before this little gathering of friends was to assemble Jeannie left Itchen Abbas for town. Victor did not go with her, for the unpunctual May-fly was already on the river, and, since subsequent days had to be abandoned, he preferred to use these. He thought it (and said so) very selfish of Jeannie to go, since who cared what gowns she wore? But it seemed that Jeannie thought this nonsense, and went. Also a tooth, though it did not ache, said that it thought it might, and she arranged an appointment in Old Burlington Street for Saturday afternoon. She would meet Victor down at Bray.

The tooth proved a false alarm. It was tapped and probed and mirrored, and she was assured that she need feel no anxiety. So in the elation of a visit to the dentist over, she emerged into the street. There was a willing but unable motor there that puffed and snorted, and did not do anything. And immediately she heard a familiar voice.

"Why, Jeannie," it said, "what confounded and stupendous luck! Never thought to meet you here. Going to Bray, aren't you? And so am I. Old Puffing Billy is having his fit here this time. Or do you think he'll have another on the road? I'll go down by train with you, or

I'll take you down in Puffing Billy. But we'll go together. By Jove, you look ripping!"

Jeannie gave him both her hands.

"Oh, Tom," she said, "what fun! Let's go down in Puffing Billy. I've been to the dentist, and there isn't anything."

Puffing Billy gave out a volume of blue smoke.

"Good old chap," said Tom sympathetically. "Hope he'll stick again on the level.—Is it all right for the present, Stanton?—Get in, Jeannie. Never saw such luck! Who would expect Puffing Billy to break down opposite a dentist's, when you needn't have gone there at all. Jove! it is good to see you."

The incredible happened. Once again the car broke down on the level, and once again Stanton had to go upon his belly, like the snake, while his passengers sat on a rug by the wayside.

"We shall be late again," said Tom. "Do you know, it is nearly six months since I saw you last?"

Jeannie remembered the invitation he had received and refused.

"That's your fault," she said.

"I know. Your man asked me. Awfully good of him."

"Why didn't you come, then?"

The inimitable Stanton ceased to be a snake, and, becoming erect, touched his cap.

"Car's all right, my lord," he said.

"Oh, is it? Get in, then.—I didn't know if you wanted me to come, Jeannie. I'm not sure if I wanted to either. But I expect the two are one. It's funny, isn't it? Try me again."

"Well, come back with Victor and me after Bray," she said.

"Rather. It's Bray first, though. We shan't be late for dinner after all. What a bore; I like being uniform and consistent. Look here, do promise me a morning or an afternoon or something down there. Just half a day alone with you."

She got into the car, he following.

"Yes, you dear," she said. "Of course you shall have it. A whole day if you like, morning and afternoon."

"Jove! I'm on in that piece. Sure you won't be bored?"

"I'll try not."

"H'm. You think it will need an effort."

Jeannie laughed.

"Once upon a time a man went out fishing for compliments—" she began.

"And he didn't catch any," said Tom.

"Not one. And now we've chattered enough, and you shall tell me all about yourself."

It was a very quiet and simple history that she heard, and all told it amounted to the fact that he had settled down as he told her nearly a year ago he was thinking of doing, but without marrying. There was little to say, and in that little he was characteristically modest. For the greater part of the year he had been down at his place in Wiltshire, of which he had been so studiously absentee a landlord, and for the first time had taken his place as a big landowner, and that which, with rather a wry face, he alluded to as a "county magnate."

It was from other sources that Jeannie knew how modest this account was, and at the end—

"Tom, you're a brick!" she said.

He laughed.

"Didn't know it," he said. "But the man who went fishing caught something after all, in that case."

Daisy came into her aunt's room when the women went upstairs that night for a talk. She was radiantly in love, but it was a different Daisy from her who had made so many plans and known her own mind so well a year ago.

"I know Willie has a cold," she said, "but men are so tiresome. They won't take reasonable care of themselves. Don't you think he looked rather run down, Aunt Jeannie?"

"Not the very slightest, I am afraid."

"How horrid of you! Oh, Aunt Jeannie, what a nice world!"

Daisy settled herself on the floor by her aunt's chair, and possessed herself of her hand.

"And to think that till less than a year ago I was quite, quite blind," she said. "I always loved you, I think, but I am so different now. What has happened, do you think?"

"I think you have grown up, my dear," said Jeannie.

"I suppose it may be that. I wonder how it happens. Do you think one grows up from inside, or does something come from outside to make one?"

"Surely it is a combination of the two. It is with us as it is with plants. From outside comes the rain and the sun, which make them grow, but all the same it is from within that this growth comes, so that they put forth leaves and flowers."

Daisy sighed.

"What a lot of time I wasted," she said. "To think that Willie was waiting so long before I could see him as he was. Yes, I know what the sun and the rain were in my case. They were you, you darling, when for my sake and poor Diana's you did what you did."

"Ah, my dear," said Jeannie, "we need not speak of that."

"But I want to just once—just to tell you that it was you who opened my eyes. And it wasn't my eyes alone you opened. It was his too—Tom's, I mean. He knows that, and he told me so."

"That is quite enough about me," said Jeannie, with decision. "Daisy, I wish Tom would marry. Can't we find some nice girl for him?"

"Oh, we can find a hundred nice girls for him," said Daisy, "and he will respectfully reject them all. He doesn't want any nice girl. Oh, Aunt Jeannie, why shouldn't I say it? He's in love with you. I think he always will be. Some people might call it sad, but I don't think it is at all. The thought of you makes him so tremendously happy."

Daisy plaited Jeannie's long white fingers in with her own.

"I think it's one of the nicest things that ever happened," she said. "It's like some old legend of a man who has—well, racketed about all his life, and then suddenly finds his ideal, which, though she is quite out of reach, entirely satisfies him. He is so fond of Uncle Victor too. That's so nice of him, and so natural, since Uncle Victor is your husband. It's just what the man in the legend would do."

Jeannie gave a long, happy sigh.

"Oh, I thank Heaven for my friends," she said.

"They thank Heaven for you," said Daisy softly.

April continued to behave with incredible amiability, and superb and sunny weather blessed Lady Nottingham's rash experiment. Everywhere the spring triumphed; on the chestnut trees below which Jeannie and Lord Lindfield had sat on the afternoon of the thunderstorm last year a million glutinous buds swelled and burst into delicate five-fingered hands of milky green; and on the beech-trunks was spread the soft green powder of minute mosses. The new grass of the year was shooting up between the older spikes, making a soft and short-piled velvet, on which the clumps of yellow crocuses broke like the dancing reflection of sun on water. Daffodils danced, too, in shady places, a company of nymphs, and the celandines were like the burnished gold of some illuminated manuscript of spring.

And all these tokens of the renewed and triumphant life of the world were but the setting to that company of happy hearts assembled by the Thames' side. The time of the singing bird had come, and their hearts were in tune with it.

The little party, so it had been originally planned, were to disperse on the Wednesday after Easter, but on the Tuesday various secret conferences were held, and with much formality a round-robin was signed and presented to Lady Nottingham, stating that her guests were so much pleased with their quarters that they unanimously wished to stop an extra day.

So they stopped an extra day, another day of burgeoning spring, and were very content. Tom was content also next morning, for he went with Jeannie to her home.

THE END.